HERO ★ 41

41

THE PEOPLE IN THE WALL

ORCHARD BOOKS
338 Euston Road, London NW1 3BH
Orchard Books Australia
Level 17/207 Kent St, Sydney, NSW 2000

A Paperback Original
First published in Great Britain in 2014

A CIP catalogue record for this book is available from
the British Library.

ISBN 978 1 40832 830 9

1 3 5 7 9 10 8 6 4 2

Printed in Great Britain

The paper and board used in this book are natural recyclable
products made from wood grown in responsibly managed forests.
The manufacturing processes conform to the environmental
regulations of the country of origin.

Orchard Books is a division of Hachette Children's Books,
an Hachette UK company

www.hachette.co.uk

HERO 41

THE PEOPLE IN THE WALL

SAM PENANT

1

There were forty of them, forty students plus me, and one of them was going to kill me. No, it wasn't a game. It wasn't a dream. It was as real as it gets. I was surrounded by knives, stacks of knives, hovering in mid-air, pointing at a part of me above the neck. Knives that in less than two seconds would hurl themselves at me and turn my head into a pin-cushion.

A knife-cushion.

It was the kind of situation that no one wants to find themselves in. That no one stands a chance of living through.

I did live through it or I wouldn't be writing this, but it wasn't because of anything I did. You see...

No, wait. I'd better start before the knife scene or it won't make sense. Two days before. Day 37 of my sentence at Scragmoor Jail.

Jail? That's right.

OK, so it isn't a jail these days. It's a school, and they've renamed it, but it still looks and feels like a jail. And guess where the students sleep.

Cells.

Yes, cells.

They call them 'bedcells' because bedcell sounds cosier than cell, but they still have the original black doors and little panels with vertical bars, and some nights, when it's quiet and dark, it's not easy to forget that prisoners used to sleep where we sleep now. And some of them never got out of there alive.

The building sits in the middle of a moor – Scrag Moor – which stretches as far as you can see in every direction but up. A huge green and brown map of the moor covers an entire wall of the Head's study. There isn't much on this map. A few tracks, a handful of ruined houses, some dips and hills and hollows and caves. But right in the centre there's this dark mass like a fist, and if you look closely you can pick out a building with a high wall round it. This is the old jail and my new school.

Scragmoor Prime.

Where a fellow student would try to murder me in very cold blood.

Before I go any further I'd better mention the Lomas Gene. The what? The Lomas Gene. Pay attention. It's called the Lomas Gene after Reinhardt Lomas, the scientist who headed the team that discovered it. It's pretty rare, this gene, and it's probably just as well that it is, because it's supposed to give those who possess it a special ability. The kind of ability that some people like to think of as a super power. All the kids sent to Scragmoor have the Gene, and quite a few had got their power by Day 37, while the rest were still waiting for theirs to show. There was just one Scragmoor student who wasn't going to get a personal power.

Me. Dax Daley.

Well that's not quite true. I did have a sort of power. The power to borrow other people's. This means that if I'm near someone with a power I get it too – usually, not always. At first, as soon as the person with the power put some distance between us their power went with them, but lately I'd started to hold on to some of the ones I'd borrowed. I didn't try to, it just happened, and let me tell you it could be pretty inconvenient.

Example.

There I am, leaning against a wall squeezing my spots, and suddenly, without planning it or wanting to, I zoom off, faster than a speeding Frisbee, or grow extra long arms, or shrink so small that I'm in danger of being crushed underfoot. These borrowed powers never last long. Few minutes at most. But a few minutes can be an awfully long time when you've just turned into a chunk of rock and you're desperate for the bathroom.

2

It was on the afternoon of Day 37 that I turned into a smoke ring. Speechless saw it happen. We were in the bedcell we share with Marcus Preedy. Marcus Preedy was called Marcus Preedy because it's his name, but Speechless was called Speechless because he doesn't speak. Not with his voice anyway. He speaks into people's minds – some people's, including mine but not Marcus's.

'Dax, what are you doing?' Speechless gasped (inside my head, as ever).

'Well, right now I seem to be flattening out on the floor,' I answered.

'How come? You've never turned to smoke before.'

'No, and I didn't want to this time. It's Damian Lee.'

'Damian? What's Damian got to do with it?'

'I rubbed shoulders with him earlier. He's got his power.'

'Turning to smoke?'

'Yes.'

'Oh, very useful.'

9

'Aren't they all?' I said.

'Some are. Rendell's speed, Marcus's flying ability, Saxon's strength.'

'Yeah, but—'

I was rudely interrupted by a shout from the corridor between the bedcells.

'I SMELL SMOKE!'

I knew that voice. It was not a voice I loved. It belonged to the Head, Dr Withering. Who threw our door back (squashing me against the wall) and demanded to know if there was a fire in here.

I kept quiet, but it wasn't easy. There's something about Doc Withering that makes me want to trade dialogue with him. And Speechless couldn't answer because the Doc's one of the many who can't hear him.

The Doc glared down at him from his great height. 'Have you been smoking?' he demanded.

Speechless put on a shocked expression and mouthed a silent 'No.'

'Smoking will stunt your growth,' the Doc said, which is a pretty silly thing to say to someone who's not much taller than a garden gnome.

Speechless made an agitated 'I haven't been smoking' gesture.

'Well, smoke doesn't just happen!' Withering said. 'Oh, wait. It's Forty-one, isn't it? Yes, if it's anyone it would be him. Where is he?'

Forty-one. That's me. He calls me that because there were supposed to be forty students at his new school but someone lobbed a spanner in the works (or couldn't count) and twenty girls and twenty boys arrived before me on enrolment day. If I'd got there earlier, someone else would have been the forty-first, but I was the last, which made me an unwanted extra in the Doc's eyes. The biggest downside of this was that there were only forty beds (bunks, that is, twenty of them) and all that was left for me was a mattress on the floor.

Typical. My life in a nutshell.

Or bedcell.

In answer to 'Oh, wait, it's Forty-one, isn't it, yes, if it's anyone it would be him, where is he?' Speechless shrugged.

'That boy,' Withering muttered. 'Nothing but trouble from the word go.'

I wanted to say 'Hey, Doc, gimme a break,' but he didn't know that I borrow other people's powers, so I stayed smoky quiet behind the door.

He turned in the doorway, and, to make sure that everyone in the entire building heard him, yelled, 'SCRAGMOOR PRIME IS A NON-SMOKING SCHOOL! IF I CATCH ANY STUDENT SMOKING, THEIR FUTURE HERE WILL BE VERY MUCH IN JEOPARDY, AND I DON'T CARE HOW SUPER THEY ARE!'

And he stormed away.

'Well, thanks a huge great fat bundle of nothing, Dax,' Speechless said when I desmoked seconds later. 'Thanks to you he thinks I'm a smoker!'

'Blame Damian. It's his power.'

'Yours too now,' he said. 'And Damian wasn't here, and you were.'

'You won't tell anyone, will you?' I said. I didn't want it getting around that I had all this stuff.

'Get me in trouble again,' he said, 'and I'll float a banner off the roof and tell the world.'

We didn't want to stay in our cell, so we headed out. Others must have had the same idea, because the stairs going down were pretty crowded. Only one kid wasn't going anywhere – Byron Flood, who just sat there, arms folded over his head while people streamed past him, nudging him and telling him to get out of the way. As usual these days, Byron had his ear-muffs on. He wore the muffs not because his ears were cold but to block out sound. Byron could hear things no one else could. Tiny sounds like mice scampering three floors away, or pins dropping.

I grabbed one of his ear-muffs and pulled it out.

'Heard anything good lately, Byron?' I yelled.

He yelped. Jerked sideways. 'Dax! Don't do that!'

I tried again, more softly. 'What's the prob, man? You look kinda stewed.'

'I'm hearing this new stuff,' he said, pressing the muff back on his ear.

'Yeah? What? Flies buzzing in a distant galaxy?'

'Groans.'

'Groans?'

'The sound people make when they could be happier.'

'Which people?' This was Speechless. Byron was one of the few who could hear him in their head.

'I don't know,' Byron said. 'It's not any of the kids, though.'

'Staff?'

'No, these are real misery groans. I mean really miserable. Wherever they're coming from, I need something thicker than these things to keep 'em out.'

He jumped up and ran down the stairs.

'Hearing like that's one power I definitely don't want,' I said.

'What are we going to do?' Speechless asked as we

hit the lobby at the bottom of the stairs.

'About what?'

'To amuse ourselves.'

'This is Scragmoor Prime,' I said. 'There are no amusements, haven't you noticed?'

'There's the games room.'

'Yeah, stuffed with games from the last century. No thanks.'

'Maybe Cat has a thought.'

Cat was just coming out of the matron's office. The matron is Mrs Withering, the Doc's wife. Cat's their adopted daughter. She saw us. Came over.

'Where are you two off to?'

'Spoilt for choice,' I said. 'You?'

'Anywhere but this building. Mum's been nagging me.'

'What for?'

'Same old, same old. Me being not just a student here but living with my parents, should help out more, bla-bla. I don't live with them. I have a bedcell, same as everyone else.'

'Mothers and daughters,' said Speechless.

She looked at him. 'What?'

15

'Mothers and daughters. They don't always agree.'

'Oh, and you're an expert on that, are you?'

'No. Just saying.'

'Well don't. I want out of here.'

'If you mean walk away never to return,' I said, 'count me in.'

'I mean out of the building, till teatime.'

So we went out the front door, down the steps, across the courtyard to the gateless gateposts. The gateposts weren't always without gates. Can't have been or the prisoners of old would have hoofed it, and who could blame them?

'So much for the sun,' Cat said.

Until now the day had been bright, with clear skies. Nice change after two days' rain. But the mist was coming in now, covering everything. It's often misty here at this time of year, they tell us. Mr Kanwar says the locals call it the Season of Mists. I don't know which locals, because Scrag Moor seems pretty much deserted apart from us. It must have been horrible in the jail years, being brought here as a prisoner, by cart or whatever, and seeing the mist get thicker and thicker the nearer you got, closing in on the place

16

you'd been sent to and were maybe never going to leave.

Because of all the rain the moor was a bit squelchy, but it was good to be beyond the wall again. There were some kids there, practising their powers: changing shape, breathing fire, levitating and so on.

'It's not fair,' said Cat.

'Now what?' I asked.

'They have powers and I don't.'

'You have eyes that glow in the dark.'

'I've always had that. I want a real power.'

'Me too,' said Speechless.

'You do telepathic stuff,' I reminded him. 'That's not exactly average.'

'Yeah, but like Cat I've always had it, so it doesn't seem special.'

'OK, you two stand here whingeing about not having a proper power. I'm going to the ruins.'

'The ruins?' Cat said. 'What for?'

I shrugged. 'Cos they're there?'

'They're out of bounds.'

'Best reason I know to pay 'em a visit,' I said.

She considered this, then nodded. 'True.'

Cat might be the Head's daughter, but she doesn't always do what she's supposed to. That's why I put up with her.

3

I'd been meaning to visit the ruins of Scragmoor
Village for a while, but I'd only looked at them from
a distance so far. People were living in the village way
before the jail was built, but not since it closed down.
It showed. Many of the cottages had crumbled and
most of the doors and roofs were gone. There was
scaffolding where men had been working. We'd been
told that some of the buildings were being restored
and strengthened for us students to use, but we
weren't suppose to go near them yet. Speechless, Cat
and I read the "Keep Out" and "Unsafe" signs very
carefully as we strolled past them.

'The builders don't seem to have done much lately,'
said Speechless.

'They haven't been back for a week,' Cat said. 'Dad's
pretty narked.'

'He's always narked about something,' I said.

'Not always. Mostly when you're about.'

An ancient chapel stood a little apart from the
cottages, as ruined as any of them and more than

19

most. You didn't realise that there were only two walls
still standing in the chapel until you went round the
first of them, which stood between the interior and
the moor. The mist seemed thicker inside the chapel
than out, but not so thick that you couldn't see that
half the roof had caved in and lay in scaggy heaps
on the floor. The other half sagged like its dearest
ambition was to come down too. The one thing
worth seeing in there was on the back wall. That wall

was actually a section of the high one that enclosed the school, and the chapel part of it was covered, end to end, with people – life-size, men mostly, but a few ladies too – trudging one behind the other. None of them looked too thrilled to have been painted, and some looked like they would kill you for your toothbrush.

'Wouldn't want to be here on a dark night with that lot,' I said.

'If it was dark you wouldn't be able to see them,' said Speechless.

'Hey, look at this,' Cat said.

She was standing beside a grey stone slab over to one side.

The slab was about two metres long by one wide and it lay on a low support wall. The slab was completely plain, but there were carved branches on the wall, writhing and tangled like they'd been caught in a high wind or storm.

'I think it's a crypt,' said Cat.

'A crypt?' I said.

'An underground vault for putting dead bodies in. Crypts I've seen before had names on them, though.

This one doesn't. It has nothing, no words, no...'

She stopped. Bent over the slab and peered at it closely.

'There is something.'

Me and Speechless looked closer too. The words were so faint that unless the light caught them just right, or you looked really hard, you'd easily miss them, like we had at first.

THEY SHALL NOT RETURN

'I don't like the sound of that,' Speechless said.

'Less worrying than "They shall return",' said Cat.

'You really think there are dead bodies down there?' I asked.

'More likely than live ones. Could be a whole family.'

'A family?'

'Miss Piper might know who,' Speechless said.

'Why would she?' Cat asked.

'She runs the school library.'

'That doesn't mean she knows everything.'

'No, but she spends a lot of time in there hoping

students will come in to borrow books, and she reads while she's waiting. She told me so.'

'I don't care who's down there,' I said. 'This place gives me the creeps.'

I went out through one of the end spaces where a wall used to be. There was a small graveyard the other side of it, dotted with little headstones. There wasn't much on most of the stones. A name, couple of dates, sometimes just a last name and death date. I noticed a little wall over to one side, with more headstones beyond it, and stepped over it to take a look.

'All the stones in this part are blank,' I said as Cat and Speechless followed me out.

'They'll be the graves of people executed at the jail,' said Speechless.

'How do you know that?'

'Because unlike you I read things. The bodies were carried straight from the Hanging Shed and dumped there without ceremony. The headstones were left blank because the authorities thought executed prisoners shouldn't be remembered.'

'Have you also read why they bothered to plant

stones if they didn't plan to put anything on them?'
I asked.

'No. But the ones over here belong to prisoners who died of natural causes, like illness or old age. Most of their bodies were brought out through an underground tunnel.'

'An underground tunn—'

'Listen!' Cat hissed suddenly.

We listened. Footsteps, coming our way, the other side of the outer wall of the chapel. Not good news on a misty day in a boneyard at the edge of an out-of-bounds ruined village. We swapped wide-eyed glances, then, all together like we'd discussed it, tiptoed back into the chapel and squatted down against the outer wall.

The footsteps were closer now, and it sounded like more than one pair.

'Maybe it's the builders,' I whispered.

'Maybe it isn't,' Cat whispered back.

We carried on crouching, expecting whoever it was to come round the wall any second and see us. But the footsteps stopped just the other side of it and someone spoke in a voice we recognised.

'My dad!' mouthed Cat.

The footsteps started up again, but heading towards the cottages. I leaned out to make sure of this and saw that the person with Dr Withering was Mr Soldoni, the Deputy Head.

'Better scarper while we can,' Cat said.

As we crept towards the end of the wall something snagged the corner of my eye on the one opposite, the one with people painted on it. I looked towards it and saw something that turned me into a statue for at least six seconds. One of the scowliest, meanest looking people on the wall turned his head, looked at me, and blinked.

Yes, blinked.

I shoved Cat and Speechless aside and was first out of there.

When I was far enough away I stopped, breathing hard, waited for them to catch up with me.

'Did you see that?' I asked.

'You running past us?' said Cat. 'Yeah, caught that. Very heroic, I thought.'

'No, I mean the wall.'

'Which wall?'

'The painted people wall. One of the people moved!'

'Moved?'

'His head. And...he blinked.'

'Blinked?'

'While scowling at me.'

Cat smirked at Speechless. And he did that corkscrew to the temple thing.

'He did!' I said. 'I saw him!'

Cat patted me on the shoulder. 'Course you did. Now why don't you go and lie down in a nice dark cell till you're over it?'

They walked on, chortling. I let them go, but glanced back at the crumbly old chapel. I'd seen it. I'd definitely seen it.

I knew I had.

4

Night. I'm in the ruined chapel. Alone. It's dark but I can still see the wall full of trudging people, and they have chains round their wrists and ankles, and one of the meanest-looking men sees me and reaches for me like he wants to do something seriously unfriendly to me. And someone shakes my shoulder.

'Eeek!'

'Dax! Wake up!'

The painted people disappeared, but it was too soon to be grateful.

'Get offa me!'

'No, listen,' Speechless said in my head. 'I'm hearing things.'

'Yes, you're hearing me say get off me, so do it please.'

'Groans. I'm picking up groans.'

'That's me being shaken awake in the middle of a sweet dream.'

'It wasn't you. You were whimpering like a little kid. It was someone else.'

'Probably Marcus,' I said. 'So wake him and let me get back to...' I thought of the man on the wall reaching for me. 'No, I'm awake now. Let's talk about raspberry jelly and party balloons and things we used to watch on telly when we were three.'

'It wasn't Marcus either,' he said.

'Speechless.' I sat up and looked at my watch. 'It's five past three, way past time for friendly chats. Go back to your bunk and stick your thumb in your gob.'

Instead of doing this he went to the door, and out. When I heard him say 'Ah!', I sighed, and got up off my lowly mattress. I looked towards Marcus's bunk, the top one. I could just make out the fact that his eyes were closed. That boy can sleep through anything.

I put my slippers and dressing gown on and went out to see what had made Speechless go 'Ah'. He wasn't the only boy in the space between the bedcells. Byron Flood was there too, and they were talking, Byron in a whisper, Speechless in his head and mine.

'I can't block them out,' Byron was saying as I joined them. 'They're even louder at night when it's so quiet.'

'I was getting the groans from him,' Speechless told me.

'Where's he getting them up from?'

'He doesn't know.'

'Will you zip it out there?' someone yelled, waking a few others.

'Downstairs,' Speechless said to the two of us.

We went out, and downstairs. We'd just made it to the lobby when Ridley Dench came out of the Infirmary. The Infirmary's where we eat our meals. It's called the Infirmary because that's what it was in the jail days. (They like to keep the old names at Scragmoor.) Ridley was rubbing his left arm with his right hand in a distracted sort of way. So distracted that he walked past us without a glance, and up the stairs. He was almost at the top when he disappeared.

Disappeared as in vanished. No big surprise. Ridley's one of the three boys whose power is to go invisible without warning.

'Friendly,' said Speechless.

'He hasn't got the invisibility under control yet,' I said.

'I mean passing us like we're not here. How are the groans now, Byron?'

'Not as bad as upstairs,' he replied.

Now that we were there, we went into the Infirmary to see if they'd left any midnight snacky stuff out. They hadn't. Not a scrap. Not a single rotten crumb. There was a biscuit and nut machine, but you needed coins for that and none of us had any loose change in our night things.

'Hey, the dungeon door,' Speechless said.

The small door at the end of the room, which led down to three floors stuffed with ancient cells and darkness and spookiness was open, which it wasn't usually. Speechless went to it.

'I wonder if Ridley was down there,' he said.

'Only crazy people would go down there at night on their own,' I said.

'He could have been sleepwalking. Sure looked like he was.'

'The groans,' Byron said suddenly.

'What about them?' I asked.

'They're louder here.'

'Hmm,' said Speechless.

'Hmm what?' I said.

'He hears the groans louder when he's upstairs near the bedcells, and here, above more cells.'

He leaned in and flicked the switch inside the door. A dim light came on, illuminating the stairs but not much below.

'Byron,' Speechless said. 'Go down there.'

Byron looked horrified. 'Down there? Me? On my own? Now?'

'Don't worry, we'll come with you.'

'We will?' I said.

'I don't want to.'

'Nor do I,' said I.

'Come on,' said Speechless, to him, not me. 'I want to see if the groans get even louder closer to the cells.'

'You might, I don't,' Byron said.

'Oh, go on. Just a step or two.'

He still hung back, but then he took a big breath and a step down, followed by another.

'Louder?' Speechless asked.

'A bit.'

'Go further.'

'I thought you were coming too.'

'We are, don't worry. Two more steps.'

Byron took two more steps. Nervous ones.

'Definitely louder,' he said. 'I don't like this.'

He turned, rushed back up. We stepped aside to make way for him, but near the top he tripped, fell sideways, landed with one ear-muff against the wall. He gasped, but stayed put for a few seconds, muff to wall, as a look of horror crept over his face.

'What?' Speechless asked him.

'Loudest yet!' Byron said.

He snapped upright, ran through the door, across the Infirmary, and out.

5

Saturday. No lessons and two whole days of free time in a place where there's absolutely nothing to do. Terrific. Cat came to sit with Speechless and me at breakfast like she does sometimes but not always.

'You look lousier than ever,' she said to me.

'My excuse is that I was up half the night,' I said. 'What's yours?'

'Why were you up half the night?'

'Ask him,' I said, glaring at Speechless.

'Why was he up half the night?'

'It wasn't half the night,' he said. 'A quarter at most.'

'Why?'

He told her about Byron, and him saying the groans he'd been hearing were louder on the steps down to the dungeons, and louder still when he had his ear to the wall, and Cat narrowed her eyes in that way of hers that she thinks makes her look intelligent.

When we'd finished plugging our chops and were on the way out, we met Byron himself, coming in. Speechless asked where he'd got to after he left us as we hadn't seen him back in his bedcell.

'Cupboard under the stairs,' he said. 'Couldn't hear much of anything with the door shut. Trouble is, I had to bang on it to be let out and no one heard me till just now. Aw, the scrambled eggs are all gone!'

We left him and trotted up to the bedcells, where Cat went her way and we went ours. After we'd done the usual bathroomy things Speechless and I went down again. Kids were swarming in and out of the Com Centre like they do every Saturday morning. The Com Centre's the only room in the entire building where there's a signal that allows us to communicate with the outside world, and it's locked every day except Saturday.

'Calling your folks?' Speechless asked me.

'Later, when the crowd's shrivelled. Maybe.'

I didn't ask if he planned to call anyone because he never does. He came to Scragmoor from an orphanage.

'Look,' he said. 'Ridley.'

Ridley was coming out of the Com Centre.

We went over to him.

'Ask him if he remembers passing us on the stairs

last night,' Speechless said. Ridley wasn't one of the ones who could hear him.

I asked, and Ridley said: 'The stairs? Last night?'

'Speechless thinks you were sleepwalking.'

'Sleepwalking? I don't sleepwalk.'

'Well someone was, and he looked a hundred and one percent like you.'

'There's no such thing as a hundred and one percent,' he said.

'What's up with your arm?' I asked. He was rubbing it.

He looked at it, like he hadn't noticed. 'It's just an itch.'

'You were rubbing it last night too, right here.'

'Not me,' he said, walking away. 'I was in bed.'

We went out the front door and stood on the steps. A few kids were in the courtyard, chatting, fooling around, practising power moves and stuff. Others just watched. We spotted Cat over by the staff transport that's parked under an old corrugated roof. She was with Miss Piper the librarian, Mrs Page-Turner – one of the teachers – and Jack Toliver, who liked us to call him Jack. Jack was the person we were supposed to go to if we had things on our minds that we needed to talk to someone about. In our first couple of weeks at Scragmoor Jack did a lot of business because some kids couldn't get used to being away from home and spending their nights in a place where people were banged up for years, and died. You'd have thought that the people who came up with the idea of turning a gloomy old prison into a school where you had to sleep in cells would have expected that sort of thing. I mean, as well as the cells, half the building was in ruins, and the shed where they used to hang people was still there – noose and trapdoor too – plus lots of other things that didn't make you immediately think of sunny days and bluebells and teddy bears.

That morning Jack was in his black leathers and crash helmet, revving his big black Harley-Davidson. He was always going off on that thing – exploring, he said, though I didn't know what there was to explore. All I'd seen around here was empty moor dotted with ponies, sheep and goats and the crumbly remains of houses that hadn't been lived in since who knows when.

As we joined Cat, Miss Piper and Mrs Page-Turner,

Jack gave a hearty wave and roared out through the gateless gateposts.

'Well that's the last we'll see of him for a while,' Miss Piper said.

Speechless and I exchanged smirks. We'd been pretty certain from the first time we saw them together that she was sweet on Jack, like he was on her. It made sense too. They were about the same age, thirty or so, the best-looking adults for miles around, and the two that everyone liked best.

'What I mean,' Miss Piper said, catching our

expressions, 'is that he'll get lost again. He's always getting lost out there on that beast of a machine, and the mist's coming in again, and...everything.'

'Don't worry, we'll send out a search party if he doesn't come back,' said Cat. 'We'll get him back for you.'

'For me?' Miss P said, all flustered. 'No, no, I don't mean...' She gave an embarrassed little laugh, 'I think I'd better go and open the library.'

'Don't bother on our account,' I said. 'We have no plans to look at books, today or ever.'

'Some of us might,' said Speechless.

'Ooh,' said Miss Piper, staring at him. 'I heard that.'

'Heard what?' asked Mrs Page-Turner.

Miss Piper, very wide-eyed, pointed at Speechless. 'Say something else,' she said.

'You really heard me?' Speechless asked.

She laughed and clapped her hands. 'You said "You really heard me?"!'

'You can hear him!' said Cat.

Speechless beamed. 'My first Scragmoor adult!'

'Why can I hear you now when I couldn't before?' Miss Piper asked.

He shrugged. 'It just happens. Or not.'

Miss was all teeth. 'I feel quite privileged,' she said. 'If you have any free time, perhaps you'll drop into the library later. I'm so thrilled.'

Laughing, she headed back to the main building with Mrs Page-Turner, who looked a bit put out that she couldn't hear Speechless too.

'Have to watch the language now you can be picked up by an adult,' I said to Speechless.

'There's Byron,' Cat said.

He was crossing the courtyard, heading for the moor.

'So what?' I asked.

'I've been thinking about those groans of his. I want to hear more about them.'

With this, she shot after him. Speechless and I eyeballed one another.

'Haven't we heard enough about his lousy groans?' I said.

'Yes. But is there anything else to do?'

'Not really.'

We went after Cat.

6

The mist was drifting in from all around the moor, kind of slyly, like it hoped no one would notice. I guessed it would take about half an hour to reach the high wall that encircles the school, which left us that much time before we needed to go back. There were some kids out there again, practising their powers or hoping to get some. Byron wasn't heading their way, but towards one of the tors (huge heaps of boulders) that are dotted all over the moor. He'd parked himself on the other side of the tor by the time we got to him, and he wasn't pleased to see us.

'I want to be alone,' he said.

'Why?' asked Cat.

'Because when I'm around other Lomas Gene kids I hear more than I want to. Like now. I knew you were coming because I could suddenly hear the grass moving, and the breathing of those sheep over there.'

'You mean if we weren't near or we didn't have the Gene you wouldn't be able to hear any better than anyone else?' I asked.

'Right. And it's getting worse, every day, every hour, so shove off.'

'We will,' said Cat. 'Soon as you've answered a couple of questions.'

'Questions?'

'These two tell me that the groans you hear are louder near the dungeons.'

He nodded. 'The dungeons and the bedcells.'

'Any idea why?'

'I think it's the walls.'

'The walls?'

'I fell against the one at the top of the dungeon steps, and it was like the groan volume was suddenly turned way up.'

'Groans in the walls...' Cat said, pulling the thoughtful look again. 'Could it be that the prisoners' misery was so heartfelt that their groans got trapped there, in the walls, like they'd been...I don't know... recorded or something?'

'Recorded by stone?' I said.

'Yes. Why not?'

'Why not because stone doesn't do recordings.'

'Oh, you know that for certain, do you, Dax?'

'Well, I...'

'No. You don't. So shut up.'

'All I know,' said Byron, 'is that I don't want to be near any cells, including the ones we sleep in. Cat?'

'What?'

'Do you think your dad would let me sleep somewhere else?'

'Somewhere else like where?'

'Like the TV lounge.'

'You could ask.'

'I will. I must. The groans are really getting to me. They're so...unhappy. I'm also sick of hearing grass and sheep, so if you don't mind...?'

'Any thoughts about the rest of the day?' I said as we stepped away from Byron's tor.

'There's some stuff I have to do for my mum,' said Cat.

'What stuff?'

'Stuff you don't need to know about. Might as well get it out of the way.'

'I promised Milton Slain that I'd teach him chess,' said Speechless.

'Chess?' I said. 'It's an old man's game.'

'It's not an old man's game. There have been chess champions of twelve and thirteen. It's a smart person's game. You'd never get into it.'

They headed back to the school. I waited till they passed through the gateless gateposts, then made for the Scragmoor Village ruins, which were even more hung with mist today. To put off what I'd come there for I went to the little graveyard first and toured the headstones that had names on them. I read a few of the names – Oliver Deeds, Harold Smint, Ella Baines, William James Lightfoot – before taking a deep breath and entering the chapel.

It was probably because I was alone this time, but the thing that hit me most about the chapel was how quiet it was. So quiet that it felt like anything could happen when you least expected it.

'Craaaaaw!'

Like that, for instance.

I looked up as a big black bird – a crow, I guess – zoomed out of the misty space that had once contained half the roof, hit the ground, and lay at my feet, not moving. Two more crows hovered way up, like they'd been fighting the first one and were

thinking of taking me on next. But they didn't take me on. They flew off. I waited for the fallen crow to move. It didn't. It just lay there, on its side, quite still. Obviously it was dead. So you have to feel sympathy for my poor spine when the bird shuddered all of a sudden, shook its feathers and jumped to its feet. I stepped sharply back, striking something with my heels as the crow took off, almost vertically, like it was going after the other two, to give them a crowish what-for.

Silence fell again, like a dead crow, and I turned to see what I'd bumped into. It was the raised slab that Cat thought was the top of a crypt. The one with the words 'They shall not return' chiselled faintly into it. Not wanting to even think about what might be beneath it, I turned, very slowly, to look at the wall full of painted people.

Now you have to picture this.

There I am, alone in a ruined chapel as silent as the graves outside, beneath hanging roof space in which black birds attack one another, a mist closing in on all sides, and I lift my head to look at this ancient wall that has life-size people painted on it, people with tormented or angry faces, some of them looking ahead of them, others looking out of the picture, and...

They weren't moving.

Or blinking.

They were just people in a painting.

I realised how stupid I'd been. Painted people don't move. They don't blink. They don't even twitch. It was this place. This cruddy old ruin. Just the kind of dump to mess with your mind and get it imagining stuff.

I laughed. Relaxed. And to prove to myself how cool I was, counted the people on the wall. There were eighteen. Six were female, the rest weren't. Eighteen painted people. Just that, painted, with brushes. Not real. I laughed again. But I'd done what I came for. Proved that I'd only imagined them moving. I don't know what I'd have done if one of them had moved suddenly.

Run out of there screaming, probably.

I was thinking this, still chuckling, when two of the meanest-looking men in the painting opened their mouths and howled with something that sounded awfully like rage, and then...then a hand of each of them came out of the wall and reached for me.

That's when I ran out of there screaming!

7

The mist was closer to the wall around the school now, and Dr Withering and Mr Gladhusband were there. Mr Gladhusband was calling everyone in, through a loudhailer.

'All students on the moor, come along now, please! We don't want anyone getting lost in the mist!'

'Well, well, Forty-one,' the Doc said as I approached. 'Doing as you're asked for once?'

'I'll start doing that as soon as you get me a bed,' I replied. 'The floor I've been sleeping on for five weeks isn't getting any softer.'

'I'm working on it,' he said.

'The floor?'

'The bed.'

'Well work on something else and let me sleep on it,' I said, strolling by.

To tell the truth, I was still a bit shaken by the howling figures on the wall, especially the one reaching for me, so it was good to be with unpainted people again. I hung about in the courtyard listening to kids talking about their powers, or each others' powers, or the powers they hoped to get soon, and it wasn't until Saxon Tull made his muscles grow to the size of footballs that I went in. Tull showing off is something I can do without *however* shaken I am.

Indoors I did something I hadn't expected to do twenty minutes earlier, or any other time. I went to the library. Miss Piper was there, but she wasn't alone.

'I thought you were chessing with Milton Slain,' I said to Speechless, the other person.

'He gave up after three minutes. Said he preferred *Angry Birds.*'

'I saw some of those out there.' He looked puzzled. I changed the subject. 'What are you doing here?'

Miss Piper answered for him, with a huge smile. 'He's communicating with me.' She tapped the side of her head.

'Right. His first Scragmoor adult. You'll soon wish you could block him out. I do, all the time.'

'Oh no, I'm thrilled,' she said. 'Truly. It's amazing to hear someone this way. Speechless and I were just...' She looked at him. 'Are you sure you want to be called that?'

He grinned. 'I'm kinda used to it.'

'We were about to test how far apart we can get before I lose him,' she told me.

'I'd like to know that too,' I said. 'Then I can move to wherever it is.'

Speechless went to the door, and out. Silence for a bit. Then I heard him say, in my head: 'Testing, testing, can you hear me?'

Miss Piper beamed. 'Yes!'

'So can I,' I said.

'I know you can,' Speechless said, looking back in.

'Go a bit further,' said Miss Piper.

He backed out again. Another bit of silence. Then: 'I'm about ten metres away. Still hear me?'

I could, as loudly as if he'd been in the room. But Miss said, 'You're fainter now.'

'OK, I'll go another few metres.'

Pause. Then Speechless said, 'How's that? One-two-three-four.'

I looked at Miss Piper. She'd gone blank. 'No?' I asked.

'Did he speak?'

'Yes.'

'And you heard him?'

'Yes.'

'Interesting that you can and I can't.'

'I've been hearing him longer. Maybe time makes a difference.'

I went to the door and told Speechless that he'd passed his cut-off point with her. 'Tell her that the range might extend as she gets used to me,' he said.

'I just did. You coming back?'

'No. Things to do. Tell her to keep tuned in.'

I turned back to Miss Piper. 'He says to tell you to tune out,' I said, and went to the shelves with books about the area.

'Looking for anything specific?' Miss asked.

'Info about Scragmoor Village,' I said. 'The ruins.'

'I know a little about the village. Not a great deal, but I've read bits and pieces in the past weeks. Feel free to test me.'

'Know anything about the old chapel?'

'Well, I know it was built in 1664,' she said.

'OK, I'm impressed.'

'Or do I mean 1764...?'

'Less impressed,' I said.

She came and stood beside me at the local shelves. Took down a book called *Life and Limb on Scrag Moor before the outbreak of The Great War.*

'Snappy title,' I said.

'It does almost rhyme, though,' she said, turning to the index at the back. She ran a finger down it, then flipped to an earlier page. 'Scragmoor Village Chapel,' she said, and held the open book out to me.

I took it. Looked at it. Awful lot of words there.

'What I'd really like to do is scroll down till I find something,' I said.

'You mean as opposed to laboriously going through the whole thing sentence by sentence until something catches your eye,' Miss Piper said.

'Exactly.'

'I could scan it for you if you like,' she said.

'Scan it?'

'Look through it. I read very quickly. Or I could see if there's anything on the computer.'

I'd seen the computer on her desk, but not thought much about it. It wasn't the most modern computer you ever saw, but if it worked...

'You can access the internet here?'

'If you're wondering why this room and no other apart from the Com Centre,' she replied, 'it's because this is where knowledge is meant to be available on request.'

She went to the desk, touched the keyboard, typed something.

'Voila!' she said seconds later. 'History of Scragmoor Village.'

I put the book back on the shelf and joined her at the desk.

'What exactly are you looking for?' she asked.

'There's this story I heard,' I answered carefully, not wanting to sound like a total loon.

'A story about...?'

'Some paintings in the chapel.'

'There are paintings in the old chapel?'

'Yes. On the wall. Of people. Eighteen of them. I wondered why they were painted.'

She keyed in the word 'paintings' but nothing was highlighted. Then she tried 'fresco' and it came up as part of 'frescoes of executed felons'.

'What's a fresco?' I asked.

'A painting on a wall. It says here...'

She read out what was on the screen, scrolling as she went. I read it at the same time.

The idea of painting likenesses of despatched prisoners on a wall of the chapel is said to have come from the prison's first governor, Mr B.L. Struthers, who, in travels before he settled in this part of the world, encountered frescoes of executed felons in ancient Egyptian temples. Governor Struthers wrote: "While I do not believe that those

executed for heinous crimes should be granted the
immortality of their names being set in stone at
the head of their graves, I am of the persuasion
that their images should be represented on a wall
in a place of worship as a warning to others who
might be tempted onto an unrighteous road."

'Pompous ass,' said Miss Piper.

I glanced at her in surprise.

'Well really,' she said, and put on a fruity I'm-in-charge sort of voice. '"I am of the persuasion that their images should be represented on a wall in a place of worship as a warning to others." I've been reading up on Scragmoor prisoners,' she added. 'Many were sent here for the most minor transgressions, and some were very unjustly dealt with in my view.'

'I'm trying to read about frescoes,' I said.

'Sorry.'

I read on.

Technically speaking, fresco plaster doesn't 'dry
out'. A chemical reaction occurs in which calcium
carbonate forms as a result of carbon dioxide

in the air combining with calcium hydrate in the wet plaster. While the practice of painting representations of hanged prisoners in the chapel ended with the retirement of Mr Struthers, a fanciful tale grew in the after-years that because the plaster was wet when each new image was added they never quite 'set', with the result that at certain times – particularly in the rather atmospheric Season of Mists – some of the figures were caught moving.

'Woh!' I said.

'What?'

I pointed to the line about figures caught moving.

'That'll be the mist,' said Miss Piper. 'Optical illusion.'

'Yeah, that'll be it,' I said.

Alongside the article there was a photo of part of the painting. It was an old black-and-white, and not a great one, but I could almost swear that some of the figures were in a slightly different position from the ones I'd seen.

'I wouldn't mind seeing that fresco,' Miss Piper said.

'Well, you know where it is.'

'Yes. But it's out of bounds.'

'Even to you?'

'To everyone, for the very good reason that any part of the village could tumble without warning.' She paused, then looked at me. 'Dax. You mustn't go there. I don't want to have to admit to the police after they find your crushed body that we had this conversation.' For a moment she looked quite stern. 'I hope that's understood?'

'Absolutely,' I said. 'This screen's the nearest I want to get to those crummy old buildings.'

So. Proof that I wasn't the only one to have seen the painted people move. Needing to tell Cat and Speechless this, I looked for them in the TV lounge and the games room and the few other places they might be, but there was no sign of them until about eleven, when I glanced outside and saw them in the courtyard with a bunch of others. They were watching a boy called Stephen Rimmer, who'd just discovered that by concentrating on light objects he could make them go wherever he wanted. He was trying this with stuff people suggested or gave him – a book, a handful of pebbles, a hat. He was new to it, so things didn't always go where he wanted them to, but he was thrilled anyway and got a few cheers.

'Wish you could do that?' I asked Speechless as I joined him and Cat.

'Throw things with my mind?' he said. 'I have hands to do that.'

Stephen carried on practising until people got bored and drifted away. Then he went too and I told

Cat and Speechless that I had something to share with them.

'Hope it's covered in chocolate,' said Cat.

'No, listen, I—'

I was cut off by the mighty roar of Jack Toliver's motorbike as he rode through the gateless gateposts. He dismounted just inside and pushed the thing the rest of the way across the bumpy cobbles.

'You think it's misty here, you should go out there,' he said to the three of us. 'I've spent the past hour feeling my way at the speed of a sloshed snail. I'm amazed I ended up here instead of somewhere else entirely.'

'I wouldn't chance it on the moor in such conditions,' said Cat.

Jack took his helmet off. 'My steed demands the exercise. But even if it didn't, I couldn't stay cooped up here all the time.'

'Some of us have no choice,' I said.

'Price you pay for being so young, Dax. It was the same for me at your tender age. No say in anything, always being told what to do. But I'm a grown-up now.' He flashed one of his big white grins. 'A grown-up with a Harley. Hard to beat!'

Then, crash helmet under one arm, he clicked his heels in the air and danced – literally danced – all the way to the steps.

'He's a nutter,' said Speechless.

'Yeah,' said Cat. 'They really hit lucky with him and Miss Piper.'

'Lucky how?'

'Dad had a hand in picking the tutors, but those two were taken on by the governors. They chose well.'

'I have an update on the fresco,' I said.

'Fresco?' said Cat.

'The painting on the wall in the old chapel.'

She curled her lip. 'Oh, your movers and blinkers.'

'I'm not the only one who's seen them,' I said.

'Oh? Who else has?'

'Well, no one here. Not now. In the past.'

'Oh, the past. I see. Always a reliable source of information, unknown people from the past.'

I turned to Speechless. 'Do you believe me?'

'A painting that moves?' he said. 'I'd kind of have to see it for myself.'

'Fine. Let's go.'

'You heard Jack. It's misty out there.'

'All right, it's misty, but we can still find our way to the chapel.'

'I can't right now,' he said. 'We're going to the dungeons.'

'What for?'

'Ask Cat. Her idea.'

I didn't need to ask her. She told me.

'Byron said the groans were louder there, especially near the walls. I want to see if we can hear anything.'

'Why would you? You don't have his super hearing.'

'You never know. We might get something.'

She spun away and made for the steps. Speechless

followed her. I was annoyed that they wouldn't hear me out, but went after them anyway.

When we got to the door to the dungeons Cat went down a couple of steps and put an ear to the wall.

'Nothing,' she said after a bunch of seconds.

'Let me,' said Speechless.

He did the same for another bunch, then shook his head.

'Like I said,' I said.

'Maybe we'll hear something down below,' said Cat.

The dungeons are on three floors, going down and down deep into the ground, which means there are no windows, no daylight. There are lights – bare bulbs, weak ones, mostly concealed, so everything's murky and shadowy. The gloom is for atmosphere. A throwback to the days when Scragmoor was a museum trying to show paying customers what it was like as an old-time prison. There wouldn't have been any electricity in the prison days, of course, but museum visitors wouldn't have had candles, lanterns or torches, so dim lightbulbs must have seemed the way to go.

Most of the other museum effects were still in place too. Such as the fake rats and cobwebs, and the life-size waxwork figures in some cells, dressed as prisoners and looking pretty peed off. They lay on iron-framed beds or sat with their heads in their hands, or at tables staring at crusts of bread or sheets of parchment. The cell walls were rough and cracked and stained, and the floors were bare stone or slate. You didn't need to half close your eyes to imagine what it must have been like here back in the day. Would have smelt different then, though. Now it just smelt damp and musty, but with hundreds of people crammed together on three floors, no windows to open, no showers or lavs or whatever, it must have ponged something awful.

'They used to have weddings here,' Speechless said.

'Weddings?' I said. 'The prisoners?'

'No, later, when it was a museum. They hired out these floors for them.'

'And what? The happy couple and their guests decked themselves out as convicts?'

'Some did. I've seen photos. Smiling faces with the cells in the background, some guests pretending to look scared or miserable.'

'Would you two mind shutting the hell up so we can listen for groans?' Cat said.

We shut up and listened.

We'd been there less than two minutes listening for groans that didn't come when, from round a shadowy corner ahead of us, we heard a creaking sound followed by movement, like shuffling feet, then a heavy door slamming.

We looked at one another. 'Sound effects?' Speechless said.

Cat shook her head. 'Most likely some of the kids,' she said, and headed for the corner that the creak, the shuffle and the slam had come round – which left me and Speechless with a choice to either stay where we were, cuddling one another with fear, or follow her.

We followed her.

The place was even more dismal round the corner. The cells were gloomier, the wax prisoners inside them looked even more depressed. Right ahead of us was the door – not a cell door, it didn't have bars or a window – that must have been the one we'd heard. There was someone in front of it. Robbie

Strogatz from bedcell 5.

'Like I said, kids,' said Cat. 'One, anyway.'

Until she spoke, Robbie was just standing there, still as a statue, but now he took a step forward, then another, and another, staring straight ahead, at nothing. Cat went to him and stood in front of him to stop him going any further.

'Robbie. What are you doing here? What's wrong with you?'

He didn't answer, or even look at her, even though she was blocking his way. He didn't seem to be aware of her. Of any of us. It wasn't till Speechless passed a hand across his eyes (Robbie's) that he jumped, and struggled to focus. Then he stared around.

'What...? How...?'

And then he did that thing he couldn't help doing when he was out of doors and the sun shone. His body lost its shape and became a puddle on the floor, running all over the heap of clothes he'd just been wearing.

'I'd probably wet myself too if I woke up down here,' said Speechless.

'You think he was asleep?' Cat asked.

'Looked like it to me.'

'I thought he could only turn to water in full sunlight,' I said.

'Maybe he wanted to see if he could do it where the sun doesn't shine.'

'You know, if there was such a thing as justice,' I said as Robbie the puddle slushed away from us, 'it would be Byron who had that power.'

'Why?' said Cat. Then she realised. 'Oh, right. Byron Flood.'

She scooped up the clothes Robbie had made all wet and we went after him, back the way we'd come. Round the corner he flowed, then to the stairs up to the Infirmary. He couldn't climb the stairs, though. Best he could do was splash against them, again and again.

'Hold these,' Cat said, shoving the wet clothes into Speechless's arms and dodging into one of the open cells.

She came back with a metal bucket. No prizes for guessing what that was used for when the place really was a prison. She took the bucket to the stairs.

'Robbie,' she said to the puddle, 'pour yourself into this. We'll carry you up.'

The puddle stopped slushing about, like it was thinking this over. Then it dived over the rim of the bucket and rippled around inside like it was trying to get comfortable, splashing droplets over the side. Funny thing, that. I'd wondered about it before. Even though drops of water break off him when he's a puddle, when Robbie gets his body back nothing's missing. You'd think a finger or toe or something even more personal would stay behind, but no, everything's still there. (So he says anyway.)

'Some help would be nice,' Cat said. 'Even as a puddle, he's no lightweight.'

It wasn't easy, but with all three of us gripping the handle we managed to get the bucket to the top of the stairs. Then we tipped it up and the puddle slopped out, changed shape, and stood up as flesh-and-blood Robbie again, quite dry but naked as a stripped banana.

'Why didn't you change back at the bottom of the stairs?' Cat asked him.

'I tried,' he said, covering his personal bits with one hand and rubbing that hand's arm with the other. 'Sometimes I can, sometimes I can't. Can I have my clothes?'

'They're wet,' said Speechless – pointlessly, as Robbie wasn't one of those that could hear him – but handed them to him anyway. Cat half turned away with a hand shielding her eyes in case they were tempted to peek – too late, the peeking had been done.

'What happened exactly?' Robbie asked as he got dressed.

'When?' Cat said from behind her hand.

'Just now, down there.'

'You turned to water.'

'I mean what was I doing there?'

'You don't know?'

'No, that's why I'm asking. First thing I knew about anything was you lot looming out of the darkness.'

'I do not loom,' Cat said indignantly. 'These two might, but I've never loomed in my life.'

I was standing a bit behind the others during all this, by the open door at the top of the stairs, when I suddenly felt like I was melting. Then I realised why. I was turning to water. Speechless glanced at where I'd been, then down at where I was, and his mouth fell open as I began to slop helplessly down the steps we'd just come up.

I heard Robbie say 'Where'd Dax go?' and Speechless say that I'd slipped back downstairs for a minute. I laughed like a drain all the way to the bottom.

I don't think.

9

Like most of my borrowed powers the latest didn't last long. I wasn't sorry. I mean there's just so much good-to-be-alive joy you can get as a puddle. My body came back seconds after I slurped onto the dungeon floor. My totally starkers body. I cold-footed it up the stairs, but stopped short of the top. Speechless kicked my clothes down to me. They were wet, but I put them on anyway.

Cat had also realised what had happened by this time, but Robbie hadn't. 'You're all wet,' he said as I rejoined them.

'I fell in water that someone left down there,' I snarled.

On the way out of the Infirmary we bumped into Cat's mum, who also noticed the wet clothes, mine and Robbie's.

'Robbie did his water stunt and splashed Dax,' Cat told her before she could even ask.

'Something wrong with your arm?' Mrs Withering asked Robbie, who was rubbing it now.

'I don't know, it just started.'

'Let me see.'

He pulled his sleeve way up and showed her the place a bicep would be if he had one. Mrs Withering said it looked like he'd been savaged by very precise gnats, and told him to come and have something put on the bites. We went too, and a few steps along Cat pulled her mother close and whispered in her ear. Mrs W looked back at Robbie, frowned, and asked her a question. Cat nodded, whispered something else, and when we got to the matron's office, said, 'We'll wait here' while her mum took Robbie inside.

'Wait for what?' I asked.

'To see what she thinks,' Cat said.

'About his arm?'

She shook her head. 'I told her about finding him in the dungeons and that he couldn't remember going there.'

There were no seats outside the office, so we leant against the wall. Speechless took out a pad and started writing in it.

'What are you writing?' I asked him after a while.

'Sentences, phrases, rhymes,' he answered.

'Nothing that means much.'

'So why write them?'

'It's something I do. You've seen me writing before.'

'I don't usually have to stand around watching you. Show me.'

He held up the pad. It was covered with words, like he'd said, but every line looked like it was written by a different hand.

'I don't get it,' I said.

'It's other people's handwriting.'

'Other people's?' said Cat, leaning sideways to take a look. Then she said, 'Speechless, that's incredible! So many different styles!'

'It's something I've done almost since I learned how to join letters up,' he said. 'When I see someone's writing I remember how it looked and write something the same way another time.'

'Another time?'

He shrugged. 'Days later...weeks...'

'You remember exactly how someone wrote weeks after you saw it?'

'It's just a thing,' he said.

'Speechless,' I said. 'You're seriously weird, you know that?'

He put the pad away. 'Yeah.'

In a while Miss Piper came along. 'What's this, a queue for Matron?' she asked.

'Mum's taking a look at Robbie's arm,' Cat told her. 'She thinks he's been bitten.'

'She buzzed me just now,' Miss said. 'Asked me to—'

Just then the door opened. 'I've put some antiseptic on his arm,' Mrs Withering said, coming out with

Robbie, 'but as he can't remember going downstairs I thought Jack should see him. Miss Piper's going to take him there. Off you go now, Robbie.'

She went back inside and Miss Piper set off with Robbie. The three of us went after them.

Jack Toliver's room had a sign on the door that said 'Jack's Joint'. Miss Piper knocked and looked in. There was a pause, then we heard her say, 'My God, you're pushing it a bit,' and Jack say, 'Bit of fun is all, no harm.'

Miss P went further in, pushed the door to, whispered a couple of things, then opened the door wider and invited Robbie in.

We kicked each others' heels for almost half an hour before the door opened and the patient stood there, as cheerful as we'd ever seen him. Jack stood behind him, also smiling.

'Whatever you do in there,' I said to him, 'save some for me.'

'Any time you hit a little hiccup, Dax, you know where I am. Robbie? Quite happy now?'

'Yeah. Totally.'

'Great. Um...' He turned to me, Cat and Speechless. 'I wonder if you three would be so good as to step in here for a minute?'

'There's nothing wrong with us,' I said.

'No, I know. I just want a word.'

Robbie toddled off on his own, beaming like he'd been given a gold-plated ice-lolly, and we went into the room.

I didn't know what to expect of Jack's office. Hadn't thought about it. A desk, maybe, a couch. But there wasn't a desk and there wasn't a couch. There were two wooden stools and – would you believe it? – a blue-and-white striped deckchair. There was also a cupboard as big as a wardrobe, and some plastic boxes, and books in a glass-fronted cabinet, and on the walls there were seven framed pictures. Three of the pictures were paintings or prints with nothing in them but colour. The other four were film posters. One of the posters was for a prehistoric comedy called *Abbot and Costello Meet Frankenstein*, one was for a film called *The Hypnotist*, and another – I forget what this one was called – showed a man in a lab coat holding a test tube. The biggest poster was for one of those action movies that has a cast of dozens, all superheroes. Jack saw us looking at these.

'Miss Piper doesn't approve of my wall decorations,' he said, glancing meaningfully at her. She stood with her back against the big cupboard, arms folded, not as smiley as usual, like she wasn't too happy with him.

'I just think that some of the subject matter isn't all it might be given what we're here for,' she said quietly.

'Well, tickles me silly, I can tell you,' Jack said. 'As you can see,' he said to us three, 'the seating's rather limited. That's because I'm supposed to talk to one student at a time, with just one other adult attending.'

'Who gets the deckchair?' I asked.

'Whoever grabs it first,' he said.

I stepped smartly forward and slotted myself into the deckchair. Cat gave me one of those 'Huh! Boys!' looks and took one of the stools. Speechless stayed on his feet. So did Jack and Miss P.

'What I wanted to ask you,' Jack said then, 'is if you saw anything that might be worth passing on to me when you came across Robbie downstairs.'

'We just found him there,' said Cat.

'Have you heard of any others in such a state?'

I felt Speechless looking at me. 'Tell him about Ridley,' he said.

'Tell him what?'

'Passing us on the stairs last night.'

'Ridley?' said Miss Piper. 'On the stairs?'

'What's that?' Jack asked her.

'Speechless said to tell you about Ridley passing them on the stairs last night,' she told him.

'Speechless?'

'It's what he likes to be called.'

'And you heard him?'

'I did.' She smiled for the first time since we'd come in. 'I have the honour of being the first grown-up at Scragmoor to hear him in my head.'

'What's this about Ridley?' Jack asked me.

'We went downstairs last night,' I said. 'Me and Speechless and Byron Flood – couldn't sleep – and Ridley Dench came out of the Infirmary and walked right by us like someone in a trance, and today he can't even remember leaving his bunk.'

Jack frowned. 'You're sure it was the Infirmary he came out of?'

'Definitely. We thought he might have gone down to the dungeons like Robbie did today.'

'Curious.' He sank onto the other stool. 'But if he did go down there...'

'Yes?' I said.

'Well, those surroundings, the shadows, the dark history of the place. A combination to play tricks on the mind if ever there was one, wouldn't you say?'

'It's probably nothing sinister,' said Miss Piper. 'Nothing *mysterious*.'

She sounded like she was trying to convince herself as much as everyone else in the room.

'Still, I wonder if we should ask Dr Withering to add the dungeons to the out of bounds list for the time being,' Jack said.

'Oh, don't do that,' said Cat. 'There's so little to do here. At least we have those floors to explore and think about.'

'Besides,' said Speechless, 'you can always put people right if they go into a trance.'

'How do you do that anyway?' I asked Jack.

'Do what?'

I repeated what Speechless had said.

'Oh, I just chat, wave my hands in front of their eyes...'

'Wave your hands?' Cat asked.

Jack smiled. 'Before I became the deeply serious person you see before you, I had a stage act that partly involved...'

He glanced at one of the film posters on the wall. The one for *The Hypnotist*.

'Bernie!' said Miss Piper sharply.

We stared at her in surprise.

'Bernie?' said Cat.

Miss Piper stared back at us for a moment, then giggled like a little girl. 'Jack. I mean Jack. I was' – she took a breath – 'thinking of someone else.'

Jack leaned forward and winked at us. 'Her ex,' he whispered.

'Ex?' said Cat.

He mouthed the word 'boyfriend', but Miss Piper caught it and looked even less pleased with him.

'You were a hypnotist?' I said. 'On stage?'

'Not only a hypnotist,' Jack said. 'I was pretty much

an all-round entertainer. Did anything likely to draw a gasp or cheer. Spot of juggling, tap-dancing, warbled a bit. I travelled all over, went to–'

'Enough now, Mr Toliver!' Miss Piper said, very firmly.

He saw that she was serious, wiped the grin off his face, and said, 'Of course. Past history and all that. What I brought you three in for was to ask you to let me know if you encounter or hear of any other students in trancelike states so that I might help them all the sooner and possibly identify the cause.'

'Can't they tell you the cause while they're hypnotised?' Cat asked.

'I asked Robbie while he was under, but he became agitated, so I soothed him into the untroubled state of mind you saw when he left here. If he does happen to remember why he went down to the dungeons, there'll be nothing in his mind to worry him about it. So if you do hear of any other cases...?'

'Hopefully there won't be any more,' said Cat.

'Hopefully. But would you keep your eyes and ears open for me, just in case?'

We said that we would, though he only heard two

replies. Miss Piper heard all three of us, of course, and beamed at Speechless like she felt really honoured.

11

Leaving Jack's office we bumped into Byron Flood coming out of Dr Withering's. He looked even less happy than earlier. When we asked why, he said he'd asked the Doc if he could pitch a tent on the moor to get away from all the noise, especially the groans, but he'd said no, absolutely not, no chance, on your skateboard kid, or words to that effect.

'I don't know what the problem is,' Byron moaned. 'There are super powers all around us. Super speed, super strength, kids turning into rocks, melting things with their eyes – all sorts of things – and I'm not allowed to pitch a tent outside the wall!'

'The problem,' said Cat, 'is that you don't have the kind of power that would help if you got into difficulties. What would you do if danger threatened?'

'Danger? What kind of danger?'

'Well, I don't know. A mad dog, a falling plane, a strolling murderer...'

'I'd hear them coming,' he said.

'I don't see how. You told us that you only have

super hearing when there are other Lomas Genes about.'

'Well, yes, true, but if another student came with me...'

'Then you wouldn't be alone any more,' said Speechless, 'which would kind of defeat the object.'

'Also,' I chipped in, 'people go missing on the moor. Someone fell down a big crack just before we started here. First anyone knew of him was when his body was discovered. They never even found out who he was.'

'They'll know who Byron is,' said Speechless.

'That's not the point,' I said.

'No, it isn't,' said Cat. 'He wouldn't be safe out there on his own. That's the point.'

'Oh, you don't understand!' Byron wailed. 'None of you understands!'

And he spun around and walked off.

I went to the front door and looked out. The mist had cleared a bit. The sun was trying to break through.

'The mist's cleared a bit,' I said. 'The sun's trying to break through.'

'Thanks for the weather update,' said Speechless.

'We could go take a look at the painted people in the chapel now,' I said.

'Oh, your blinking movers,' said Cat.

'They don't just blink,' I said. 'Their arms come out of the wall.'

She folded her own arms and gave me one of her superior looks.

'Oh,' she said. 'Really.'

'Yes,' I said. 'Really. So what do you say?'

'I say I have better things to do.'

'Oh yes, like what?'

'Like almost anything. If I want to see moving people I look around me.'

I turned to Speechless. 'What about you?'

'Lunch soon,' he said.

'This is more important than lunch,' I said.

'Not to me.'

I gave them both the scowl I perfected in mirrors when I was young.

'All right, I get it. I'm on my own. Thanks – friends.'

I yanked the front door back and stomped down the steps.

I didn't need to go back to the chapel as they weren't coming with me, but I crossed the courtyard anyway, in case they were watching. But as I turned left out of the gateless gateposts, an enormous sheet of paper flapped out of nowhere and wrapped itself around me. I fell back against the wall, thoroughly wrapped – until the paper fell away from me and turned into Elinor Ruffgarden.

'Sorry, Dax,' Elinor said. 'Practising.'

'Practising being a bit of paper?' I said. 'That must be hard.'

'It's not my fault that it's my power,' she said.

'I didn't ask for it.'

'No,' I said. 'Right. So what's to practise?'

'I wanted to see what I could do as paper.'

'And?'

'I can lie down. I can fly a little.'

'That must feel very rewarding,' I said.

She looked kind of downcast. 'Not too impressive, is it?'

I suddenly felt sorry for her. 'It could be worse. Think of George Bergoglio. Twice normal height, yellow, icy breath. What can you do with that?'

'You could frighten baddies,' she said.

'Or Diane Bentley. Snakes on her head. Says they ruin her hairstyle.'

'At least snakes can spit. Enemies might not like to be spat at by snakes. What could a sheet of paper do?'

'It could wrap 'em up,' I said. 'You just proved that.'

'Mm...' she said. 'I suppose if I can become really strong paper I might be able to contain them...keep them prisoner for a while.'

'Yeah, could be useful. So keep working on the paper strength.'

Her face brightened. 'I will,' she said, 'I will,' and she wandered off to practise the paper thing some more.

Without really thinking about it, I carried on the way I'd started going, and was almost at the chapel before I realised and lurched to a halt. I thought of the people on the wall. Cat and Speechless might not believe me, but I knew they'd moved. Two of them anyway. Their arms had come right out of the wall like they wanted to grab me. What would have happened if they had? All eighteen of those people must have been hanged back in the jail days, or likenesses of them wouldn't have been put on the wall, and the two who'd reached for me didn't look the types that would have been hanged for flower arranging. If they'd been murderers, they might want to go back to their old ways, and murder me.

Could paintings that came to life do that?

I didn't know, but I wasn't sure I wanted to test it. I didn't need to. I mean I was the only who'd seen the people move. If I didn't go back there, they could dance a tango and no one would know.

So. Turn around, Dax Daley. Go back the way you came. Forget about paintings moving and doing stuff.

88

I was about to do that very thing when I remembered that I was supposed to be a hero, or was expected to be someday, and that heroes – even future ones – don't turn from little things like paintings wanting to kill them. No, they stick out their chests and clench their jaws and go on, primed for trouble.

So I went on, saying over and over in my head, 'I'm a hero, I'm a hero, I'm Hero 41, and one day I'm gonna fight crime and terrorism for SH1.'

Have I mentioned SH1? No? Well, it's the government department behind Scragmoor Prime. We'd been told that those of us who graduate at sixteen or so with fully developed powers will be offered a job working for them as superheroes. Yes, actual superheroes, with a Licence to be Super in Public. Sounds insane? That's what I thought too, originally, but I've got used to it. None of us had done anything heroic yet, of course, but the tutors were already calling us heroes, probably to boost our little egos, and as I'd been the forty-first student to arrive on enrolment day I was Hero 41. And as Hero 41, I could hardly run from people in a painting, now could I?

While the mist had thinned out almost everywhere else by now, it still hung around the chapel, which made it look pretty spooky. But (chest out, jaw clenched) I went in anyway and this time made myself look at the fresco on the wall right away. The line of people, trudging one behind the other like they were heading home after a hard day at the noose, looked as grim or mean as ever, but none of them were moving, or doing anything at all.

Until the groans started.

When I heard them, my hair reached for the skies and my heart jumped up to my throat and tried to shove its way out. Now the people were moving. Not all of them, just three or four. Their heads were turning, their mouths were opening, and it was from those mouths that the groans came.

As I stood seeing and hearing all this, hair bolt upright, heart in mouth, I remembered that when Byron Flood said the groans on the dungeon steps were louder close to the wall, Cat wondered if they'd been trapped there since the prison days, locked into the stone, heard by no one till he came along all these years later. Well, I'd been in contact with Byron. I'd absorbed his hearing power without knowing it. A power which, like the others I'd borrowed, became active when it felt like it – like now, standing in front of the painted people wall. The painted people who were not only groaning, but...

... looking at me!

Shocked, horrified, all the rest of it, I jumped back, way back, well away from the wall, and...the groans ceased...the mouths stopped moving...the heads turned back to where they'd been before, and froze again.

Too stunned to be relieved, it took a few secs for me to notice the other voices. Voices, from behind me, the other side of the outer wall.

One of which was Dr Withering's.

I cast about for somewhere to hide. There wasn't a huge amount of choice. In fact, none. Panicking a little, I took one of those dithery backward steps you take when you don't know what else to do with your feet, and my heel struck something, which made me sit down hard. I looked to see what I'd parked myself on. It was the 'They shall not return' slab. And it wasn't quite closed. I was sure it had been closed last time I looked, so I reckoned I must have caused it to move when I sat down so heavily. At any other time I might have shivered at the thought of what was beneath the slightly open slab, but I had something else to think about now: Doc Withering and whoever was with him finding me where I shouldn't be. That would mean a lecture. I wasn't in the mood for lectures. I wanted to be somewhere else entirely. Anywhere at all but there.

I was just thinking this when my body thinned out and changed shape and became a sheet of paper that

slipped through the gap at the edge of the slab, and floated down into the pitch black space below.

The crypt.

And landed on something soft.

12

I don't know where my eyes and ears could have been in a sheet of paper, any more than I knew where they'd been in a pool of water, but it was business as usual with the hearing and seeing. I couldn't see much in all that darkness, of course, and as for the hearing thing, all I could make out was the two voices up above, now very near where I'd floated down from. I just lay there thinking that being able to turn into paper could have its uses and that I would have to pass that on to Elinor Ruffgarden next time she wrapped herself around me. The news might cheer her up.

So there I was, lying in a crypt under an ancient chapel with the only light coming from the thin crack I'd fallen through. The crack didn't let in enough light to show any part of my surroundings, but that wasn't necessarily a bad thing. I mean crypts have coffins in them, and in films the coffins open when visitors drop in, and the people in them sit up. Quite often the people who sit up don't have a whole lot of flesh on their bones, but they still manage to climb out and advance on the visitors in an unfriendly sort of way.

That's what I imagined the people in the coffins all around me in the total darkness were doing as I lay there doing a fine impression of a sheet of paper. And guess what. I wasn't terrifically comfortable with that picture in my paper head. I was even tempted to shout for help, and I might have too, except that even though I could see (not much) and hear (not much more) I didn't seem to have a mouth to shout with. So I just listened, and what I heard was the voice of the person who'd entered the chapel with Dr Withering. Mr Soldoni. Again. I couldn't make out what they were saying, but Mr S didn't sound as cheerful as usual, and the Doc...well, he sounded about standard for him, crotchety as a crocodile waiting to be stuffed.

But then they drifted away, and as they went I gave a papery flutter (without trying) and turned back into flesh and blood (my own, I'm glad to say). I sat up, wondering how I would get out of there, and as I thought this my eyes switched on. I mean actually switched on, like a couple of eyeball-size bulbs. This had only happened once before, in another very dark place, when I was with Cat.* Like Cat's, the glow from my eyes was green, but that was all right. Even green light can help you see in the dark.

If you want to.

More than half dreading what my green peepers would reveal, I looked nervously around me – and breathed a hefty sigh of relief. No advancing fleshless figures. No coffins. Just a room with a couple of chairs and a cupboard. There was also a trolley with some equipment on it – test tubes, glass beakers, a measuring jug, a blue box with some wires – the sort of stuff a kid might set up in his bedroom to see if he can turn cotton wool into gold or chocolate. There was also a laptop and a thermos flask. The laptop and thermos looked new, even in that light. But I was more interested in what was I sitting on. I slipped off it and saw that it was a bed. A bed on wheels. A hospital-type bed. No blankets, though, no duvet, not even a pillow. Just a white sheet over a thin mattress.

* *See* Eye of the Gargoyle, *Dax's first adventure at Scragmoor Prime.*

After the bed I noticed two other things. One was a set of stone steps up to the crack I'd fallen through. The other was a door on the other side of the room. I went to the door and reached for the handle. But paused. I had no idea what might be the other side of that door. Could be anything. Anything at all.

But then I remembered that I was Hero 41. Afraid of nothing.

In theory.

I opened the door with my green eyes shut, and waited for a fist to come at me or a howling monster to rip my head off.

But nothing happened. I opened my eyes, lash by lash, and squinted at...

Complete and utter darkness.

Complete, that is, if you don't count a low ceiling and walls about a metre and a half apart that look like they've been chipped out of rock with nail files. My green eyelight wasn't tremendously powerful, so I couldn't see far, but it looked like a tunnel. I remembered what Speechless said about the jailers of old carrying dead prisoners to the chapel from the dungeons. The gap that I'd dived through as a sheet of paper was in the chapel, so it could be that this was that tunnel. If it was, it would take me to the dungeons under the school, and from there I'd be able to get up into the main building.

I took a step forward.

And the light in my eyes died.

Like I said before, one of the problems with these borrowed powers is that they don't last. Another is that I can't pick and choose which ones I get, or when. I dread suddenly shooting up into the sky like Marcus Preedy and just as I reach the clouds there's a flying power cut. The only thing left to do if that happened would be to scream head-first all the way back to the ground, where I'd end up resembling a ripe tomato squashed by a stampeding elephant.

I stood in the doorway for a minute, blinking hard, muttering, 'Come on, eyes, do your stuff, light up, light up!' But they stayed unlit. So I reached out, touched the nearest wall, took a cautious step forward. Before my eyes went out I'd seen that there was nothing immediately ahead of me, but that didn't mean there wasn't. I took another step, then another, holding on to the wall with one hand, the other out before me to stop anything unexpected coming at me. In that darkness, even a cobweb might have brought a little shriek.

I'd gone no more than five paces when they started.

Groans, just ahead of me.

Groans of men, women and children.

Groans of misery and fear.

I stopped walking. Well, wouldn't you? But even though I'd stopped, the groans came closer, and closer, and grew louder, and louder, and increased in number. I might have turned and run, but for some reason my feet wouldn't move. (This is something that happens to my feet in times of crisis, don't ask me why.) Then the groans were all about me, in the walls and ceiling and floor, and... I'm not sure, because there was no one there to take a picture of me, but if there wasn't a nice relaxed smile on my face there might have been one of blind, wide-eyed terror.

Standing there in the darkness, the groans filling the tunnel and my head, I couldn't help imagining bodies being carried towards me, the bodies of dead prisoners, and I sank to the ground, right up against the wall, arms over my head, groaning groans of my own.

I was still squatting there when I felt something happening to my body, like it was folding in upon itself, curling over and...round.

And then...

I started to bounce.

Yes, bounce.

I bounced and bounced along the tunnel of groans, hitting the walls, the ceiling, the floor, and somewhere in all this groany bouncing realised that I was using Josh Silverman's power. I'd crashed into Josh the day before as he bounced out of the bathroom. Literally bounced. Josh's power was turning himself into a ball. So far he'd managed to become a football, a basketball, a rugby ball and a tennis ball. Obviously I'd absorbed his power without realising it – and become a beach ball.

After what felt like an endless bounce along the tunnel I struck something that made a soft, dull clang, and bounced off it, instantly becoming myself again just in time to land on my rear end for the second time in minutes. As I sat clawing some breath back after all the bouncing in the dark, I realised that the groans had also stopped. But then I heard another sound.

Knocking.

It seemed to be coming from the thing I'd bounced off. I crept forward on hands and knees, feeling the grit of ages under my palms, until I could touch it and feel around it. It was a door. Had to be. And it was still being knocked on, on the other side.

And then I heard a voice – in my head.

'Dax? You there? Knock twice for yes, three times for no.'

101

I stood up and rapped twice on the door.

'Great,' the voice in my head said. 'Now. Can you talk?'

'YES!' I shouted.

'Was that a yes?'

'YES!!!'

'What are you doing in there?'

'SHOUTING AT YOU!!!'

'I mean why are you there?'

'CAN WE DISCUSS THAT WHEN I'M THE OTHER SIDE OF THIS DOOR?!'

'OK. Can you unlock it?'

'NO!!!'

'All right, there's no need to shout.'

'I'M SHOUTING BECAUSE YOU CAN'T HEAR ME!!'

'You're coming through more clearly now. Is there a key, or a bolt or something?'

'I DON'T KN...' I lowered my voice. 'I don't know. I can't see a thing.'

'Well feel around.'

'I am. Can't find a bolt. There's a handle and a lock, but no key.'

'Feel round the edges.'

'Edges of what?'

'The door.'

I felt round the edges of the door. And found a big key on a hook.

'How did you know there'd be a key on a hook?'

'I didn't, it's just that sort of door. Put it in the lock. The key, not the hook.'

I unhooked the key, dropped it, swore, got down on my knees again, felt around. When I found the key I folded my fingers tightly round it so I wouldn't drop it again, got up, and spent the next fifteen hours trying to fit the useful end into the keyhole. Then I turned it, and after a couple of clunks as the lock's internal workings rolled over, I turned the handle and pushed.

The door didn't open!

So I pulled it.

And it did.

'Hi, Dax,' said Speechless on the other side.

'That goes for me too,' said Cat, who was with him.

'How did you know I was in there?' I asked them.

'He sensed you,' said Cat.

'Sensed me? When? Where?'

'We were at lunch,' Speechless said, 'and I got this sudden feeling that you were in some sort of difficulty somewhere below us, so we snuck down here, and the feeling drew me to this door.'

'Speechless,' I said, 'I don't care what you say, that's

definitely a power you have there. I mean how many people can sense things like that long distance?'

'And spoil my lunch,' grumbled Cat.

'I'm still hoping I'll get something more impressive,' Speechless said.

'What, like Tull with his stupid muscles?'

'I'd be happy with just one stupid muscle.'

'What's in there?' Cat asked, nodding into the blackness behind me.

'A tunnel,' I said. 'Obviously the one they took the bodies to the chapel through in the good old days.'

'The chapel's at the other end?'

'Yes.'

'I didn't see anywhere that a tunnel could come out.'

'It ends at the room under the slab you thought was a crypt. Now we know what "They shall not return" means. That it's a one-way trip, ending there.'

I started to close the door.

'What about the key?' Cat asked.

'It's in the lock on the other side.'

'Well you can't leave it there.'

'Why not?'

'Because it wasn't there before.'

I stepped back into the tunnel, took the key out of the lock, hung it on the hook, and closed the door behind me.

'Now it's not locked,' said Cat.

'So what do you suggest?' I said. 'I lock the door from the inside, put the key back on the hook, and squeeze myself out through the keyhole?'

She narrowed her eyes at me. 'And you wonder why my dad has a problem with you?' she said.

Then she went into the nearest cell that had an open door and told us to come too. I asked what for.

'For you to tell us what you were doing in there.'

She sat on the bed, and so did Speechless. I didn't sit.

I got as far as telling them how I'd turned into a sheet of paper and a beach ball before I had to threaten to lock Speechless in the tunnel and drop the key down a drain if he didn't quit laughing. It still took him a minute to dry his eyes and get his face more or less straight.

'It's interesting, though,' said Cat, who hadn't joined in the hysterics.

'What is?'

'If you hadn't turned paper-thin you couldn't have got down a really narrow gap, and if the tunnel goes all the way from here to the chapel what could be a handier way of getting along it than as a bouncing ball?'

'A bowling ball would have been better. All that bouncing's given me a headache.'

'What I'm saying,' she said, 'is that the right powers kicked in when you most needed them, without you even trying to...call them up or whatever.'

'I wouldn't know how to anyway,' I said.

'Yeah, but you see what I'm getting at? The powers you've borrowed from other people seem to self-activate when needed.'

I remembered how my eyes had glowed in the dark below the slab – I hadn't mentioned that – and was about to admit that she might have a point when she changed the subject.

'You really heard groans in there?'

'Yeah. Loads of 'em. Groan upon groan, with echoes.'

'So Byron isn't imagining them.'

'I didn't know you thought he was. I know you doubted me, but not him.'

'Doubted you?'

'About the moving figures on the chapel wall.'

'Oh, don't start that again.'

'See what I mean?'

She slapped her knees and stood up. 'Well, if that's it, I said I'd play *Twilight Imperium* with Sofia Papalia and a couple of others.'

'In case you're interested,' I said, 'and I know you're not, the groans weren't only in the tunnel.'

'What do you mean?'

'I heard the wall people groan too.'

'Of course you did,' she said with a sigh.

'Don't you want to hear about the room under the chapel?' I asked as she went to the cell door.

She paused. 'Depends how interesting it is.'

I told them about the things in the room.

'Scientific equipment and a bed on wheels?' said Speechless.

'Very basic scientific equipment,' I said.

'Perhaps it was a mini morgue in the prison days,' said Cat.

'There was also a thermos flask and a laptop. They didn't have things like that back then.'

'They could have been left behind by the people who ran the museum.'

I shook my head. 'The museum closed years ago and the flask and laptop weren't even dusty.'

'You didn't look in the laptop?'

'No, the lid was down.'

'You could have lifted it.'

'Other things on my mind, like getting out of there.'

'And that's what I'm doing here, now,' Cat said, and she left.

I also started to leave, but Speechless asked me to wait a minute.

'What for?'

'Checklist,' he said.

'Checklist?'

He held up a fist and one after the other raised his thumb and fingers as he listed things.

'You've found the tunnel the jailers carried dead bodies through for burial in that graveyard. And a room with a bed and equipment that sounds like it's been used recently. Twice we've seen people in

a trancelike state in these dungeons – or maybe coming out of them in Ridley Dench's case – and we heard a door close when Robbie Strogatz was down here, which might have been the door to the tunnel. Also, you heard groans, like Byron does.' He closed his hand. 'Anything strike you about all that?'

'Yes. You have four fingers and a thumb on that hand, congratulations, let's go.'

'No, hang on. I mean they could all be linked. Students are put into a trance and taken to that room, where something's done to them before they're turned out with that bit of their memory erased. And Ridley and Robbie had itchy left arms. I don't know if it was the same for Ridley, but Mrs Withering thought Robbie'd been bitten by gnats. Well, I'm thinking needles, not gnats.'

'Needles?'

'From an experiment in the room under the chapel.'

'You think they've been injected with something?'

'Could be.'

'That's a bit serious,' I said.

'Who says it has to be funny?'

'No, right, but...needles? You don't think you're letting your imagination go a bit too far?'

'No, Dax,' he said. 'I'm using it. You should try taking your imagination for a walk sometime. You never know. Might stumble across something worth thinking about among all the garbage.'

He pushed past me and headed out.

14

About 2.30 that afternoon Power Saturday started. They call it Power Saturday because it doesn't take place on Sunday, Monday, Tuesday, Wednesday, Thursday or the other one. It doesn't happen every Saturday either. This was only the fourth since we started at Scragmoor. The idea is that the students are taken out to the moor (far enough from the school so we can't damage the cruddy building) and the ones who have found their powers, or developed them a bit since last time, can show off to the rest of us. I'd got out of any demonstrations so far by keeping quiet about my unwanted ability to borrow other people's and asking the few who knew about it to keep their traps shut too. Like me, Cat and Speechless hadn't owned up to having a power, but that was because they didn't think they had one yet.

I managed to grab a couple of sausage rolls by being nice to Mrs Beverage the head cook and nodding sympathetically while she told me the tragic life story of every single member of her family.

Then I got myself a power bar (ho-ho) and trailed after all the others swarming out to the moor with Mr Cosmo, Miss Niffenegger, Mr Gladhusband and Ms Samson. These four are our 'super tutors'. They're called that because years ago they had the idea of making themselves wacky superhero type costumes and patrolling the streets at night to try and stop people doing things like car-jacking, house-breaking, dropping litter and so on. According to them it worked pretty well until the police told them to hang up their nut-job cozzies and stick to the day jobs, teaching English, Biology, PE, Geography and History. But a few years later, when the Lomas Gene was discovered and the idea of a school for future superheroes popped into some lunatic's mind, SH1 offered them the jobs they had now because it was thought they would have a better idea than most of how to prance around like heroic prats. On Power Saturdays Mr Cosmo, Miss Niffenegger, Mr Gladhusband and Ms Samson squeezed themselves back into their old tights and capes and masks and so on, which was pretty embarrassing really.

As usual we were taken to the big open area to

the right of the road in case someone accidentally toppled a tor on someone else.

'Can't see Cat,' Speechless said.

'Why do you want to?' I asked.

'No reason, just wondering where she is.'

'She and Sofia probably fell asleep playing that game.'

'If they did, Sofia woke up and left her with her head down.'

He nodded into the crowd. Sofia was there with some friends and Cat wasn't one of them.

The four super tutors asked everyone to stop fooling around (some were) and for those who had a power to come to the front and take turns showing what they could do. My cue to nip round the back and try not to be noticed. Speechless nipped with me. Someone already at the back was Byron Flood, who'd been out here on his own before everyone arrived. He was still wearing his ear-muffs, with extra padding between his ears and the muffs, and he still looked miserable.

'Can you hear me?' I whispered from about six metres away.

'Stop shouting!' he said, and ran to a distant tor, and behind it.

'He did say it's worse when there's a lot of us about,' Speechless said.

From the back we couldn't see everything that was going on at the front, but we caught a few things, including one I would have been happy to miss: Saxon Tull performing. In the past few weeks Tull had learnt to grow his muscles whenever he liked, and lift things too heavy for any sane person to even want to lift. Right now he was holding a huge boulder over his head, which got cheers from his airhead fan club.

Others demonstrating their powers included two of the three boys who could vanish into thin air, Tamsin Gorey shape-shifting into a fridge, Diane Bentley feeding the snakes in her hair with Smarties, and Marcus Preedy zooming up almost to the clouds and drifting gently down. Then there was Scarlett O'Mara, who created a mist around herself but shouted for help when she couldn't find her way out, and Rendell Bude doing a speed-of-light dash across the moor (his power fizzled out five miles away and he had to walk back). One boy – Azio Mazawa – stepped forward claiming to be seeing ghosts all round us, but as no one else could see them it was hard to tell if he was just seeking attention.

'Holy Moly, look at Eric!' someone shouted.

Eric Blair was one of those who hadn't had a power before, but all of a sudden he had two extra heads, one on each shoulder, identical to the one in the middle. A few of us found this hilarious. I was still laughing when I picked up a stereo echo and Speechless said, 'Dax...' in a high, strangled sort of voice.

'What?' I asked, again with a stereo echo.

'Look to your right.'

I looked to my right. I was nose-to-nose with a face just like mine.

'And your left.'

I looked to my left. Another twin. Or triplet.

I ducked into a crouch before anyone could see me.

'Two extra heads?' my three heads whispered. 'How can the ability to grow two extra identical heads be a power?'

Speechless squatted down with me. 'I've been

thinking about that. Not extra heads. The power
thing. Could be that "power" isn't the right word.'

'You could say that,' my three mouths said. 'And
again and again, even.'

'No, I mean the *word* power. Some of the students
have got a definite power – Saxon, Rendell, Tamsin,
Marcus, a few others – but hair becoming snakes like
Diane's? Things turning to gold when Bonnie Bodine
touches them? George Bergoglio growing to twice
his normal height, turning yellow and breathing ice?
They sound more like mutations than powers.'

'If you're thinking X-Men,' I said with a single
voice as the stand-ins on my shoulders shrivelled

back where they came from, 'they don't need to worry about competition from us.'

'The Lomas Gene has to be a mutation,' he said. 'I mean it's hardly normal or everyone would have it. I'm betting that Reinhardt Lomas knew that, but SH1 didn't want it called a mutation in case we thought we were freaks or something.'

'Which we are,' I said.

I stood up – and was instantly surrounded by a mist like Scarlett O'Mara's.

'Why me?!' I wailed from the heart of the mist. 'What have I done to deserve every stinking crummy power going?'

'Mutation,' said Speechless, from somewhere in the mist.

'Call it what you like, I wish you had it rather than me.'

'Good thing wishes aren't one of the mutations,' he said.

'I'd say watch this space,' I said, 'but you can't see it right now.'

The mist cleared seconds later, leaving me gazing gratefully at the nice clear view across the moor, part of which was a car that hadn't been there before, heading our way.

'Hello,' said Speechless. 'What would the rozzers want out here?'

The police car pulled up as near as it could to us and two uniformed coppers got out, one man, one woman. As they walked towards us, the tutors told the ones who'd been demonstrating their powers (or mutations) to do nothing out of the ordinary. This meant that when the cops arrived the only ones who didn't look normal were the tutors themselves. Mr Gladhusband greeted them and asked if they'd come to watch our 'fun day'.

'Fun day?' the male police person said. 'Well, that accounts for your outfits. Don't the kids get any?'

'They have yet to make them,' said Ms Samson, doing one of her hugely embarrassing arms-in-the-air twirls. 'But if you'd like to brighten yours up...'

'I think we'll stick with boring,' said the policewoman, smirking at Ms Samson's too-tight tights.

They told us that a retired couple hadn't been seen since they set out on a hike across the moor three days ago and the owner of the B & B they were staying at had alerted the police. Search parties were now combing other parts of the moor and the policeman and policewoman wanted to know if the school would help by searching this part. Mr Cosmo called Dr Withering and got his approval for us to do that, and the police warned us to be careful where we walked, and drove back the way they'd come.

15

There was quite a buzz among the students. Searching for missing hikers sounded like a nice change from our usual weekend activities. Miss Niffenegger suggested that we divide ourselves into four groups, each with a tutor, and go in different directions, and the other tutors agreed.

'No wandering off on your own, though,' said Mr Cosmo. 'We don't want to have to search for some of you too.'

'Why don't I fly out there and have a look for these people?' Marcus Preedy suggested.

'Probably not such a good idea,' said Mr Gladhusband, 'seeing as you don't also have the power to make yourself invisible and there are police and search parties all over the moor who might notice you.'

'And the cops might shoot you down,' said Saxon Tull.

'Wish someone'd shoot you down,' I muttered – not quietly enough, but at least when he came

121

back with 'I heard that, Daley' it gave me a chance to say, 'Hey, not only big fat muscles but big fat ears – round of applause for our top naff hero, everyone!'

No one applauded.

'The world is unaware of the purpose of Scragmoor Prime and what any of you can do,' said Mr Cosmo, following on from what Mr Gladhusband said. 'So we must insist that students with powers resist the urge to use them if there's the slightest chance of your being observed.'

A peeved mutter went up from those who'd started to look forward to using their powers for something useful for the first time.

In school we're divided into four class groups – three of ten, one of eleven – but for the search many of us went to stand with people we wanted to be with, never mind which group we're usually in. This meant that two groups had too many and the other two had too few, so the tutors did a bit of rearranging, until three of the groups were more or less equal, and only one – the one me and Speechless were in – was a bit larger. This turned out to be handy because as the four groups set off in different directions, we saw

Cat in the distance and fell back and let ours go off without us.

'What's she doing over there?' Speechless said.

She was wandering out of the ruins of Scragmoor Village, towards the school. After checking to see that none of the tutors were looking back, we ran to her.

'What were you doing down there?' I asked her.

She walked past us without a word or glance.

'Uh?' said Speechless.

'My next question exactly,' I said.

He ran round in front of her to stop her going any further. She stopped but didn't look at him.

'Cat?' he said.

No reply. No response of any kind.

'There's something wrong with her,' Speechless said.

'Nah, she's fooling around.'

'Oh yes? Doesn't this remind you of anyone?'

'You don't mean...'

'I do.'

'Pinch her,' I said.

'Pinch her?'

'Her arm or something.'

'You pinch her.'

I pinched the top of her arm. She winced but still didn't say anything or look at me.

'We ought to take her to her mum,' I said.

Speechless agreed, and we walked her – one on each side – towards the gateless gateposts. We were almost there when I happened to glance back at the ruins and see Miss Piper coming out of the chapel.

'You take her,' I said to Speechless. 'Someone I want to speak to.'

When Miss Piper saw me coming at a trot she looked surprised first of all. 'What,' she said, 'not participating in Power Saturday?'

'It was cut short,' I said. 'The cops came.'

Her eyes widened. 'The cops? The police? What for?'

'Two people have gone missing on the moor and they wanted help to look for them. Everyone's gone except me and Speechless because we found Cat in a sort of trance, and Speechless is taking her to her mum.'

'A trance?' Miss Piper said. 'Like Robbie?'

'And Ridley. She was coming from down there, where you were. You didn't see her there?'

Miss glanced back at the ruins. 'I was nosing round the cottages. Couldn't resist after our chat about them. Finally went to the chapel to look at the fresco, but before I could take some snaps on my phone I heard voices and left in a hurry.'

'Voices? From the wall?'

She laughed. 'The wall? No. I couldn't make out who it was or if I knew them, but I shouldn't have been there, so I made a swift departure. I do wish I'd seen Cat, though. I might have been able to do something.'

'The people on the wall...' I said.

'Oh, Dax, they're amazing. So lifelike!'

'Oh yes? You didn't see them...move?'

She laughed again. 'No such luck.'

We walked slowly back to the school. Crossing the courtyard we found Cat and Speechless sitting on the steps up to the front door. Cat was gazing about her in a puzzled sort of way like she couldn't get a handle on where she was. And she was holding her arm where I'd pinched it.

'Mrs Withering wasn't in her office,' Speechless said as we approached.

'She should be somewhere in the building,' Miss Piper said. 'I'll go and see if I can find her.'

'What do we do with Cat while you're gone?' I asked.

'How about taking her to the games room?'

'You don't think we should get Jack to take

a look at her?'

'Might be an idea. I'll see if I can locate him too.'

16

We didn't have long to wait in the games room. I'd only dissed half the games on display when Mrs Withering appeared in the doorway, saw us, and flew over like someone wearing wings.

'I've just met Miss Piper,' she said. 'What's wrong with Cat?'

We started to go through the 'we-don't-know-we-found-her-like-this' routine, but she wasn't listening. She was on her knees holding Cat's hand and stroking her hair and trying to get her to look at her and answer a torrent of questions.

Jack came in a few minutes later, with Miss Piper. Mrs Withering agreed that he should see if he could pull Cat out of whatever she was in, and we went to his office, all of us. Mrs W asked if she could go in with them, but Jack said, 'Best not. Loved ones present during sessions can have a destabilising effect on the subject as they start to come out of a condition like this.'

'What is this condition?' she asked.

'That has yet to be determined,' he replied. 'But I'm wondering, as Cat isn't the first to come down with something like this...is it Scragmoor, perhaps?'

'Scragmoor? I don't understand.'

'History-rich premises have been known to unsettle impressionable minds, and Scragmoor certainly has a history. Miss Piper can come in. She's not emotionally involved and has seen me do this before.'

They took Cat into Jack's office and Mrs Withering went to find her husband. He wasn't in his study just along the corridor, but about ten minutes later she appeared with him. They didn't join Speechless and me but kept to the lobby, walking back and forth looking worried, glancing every so often to where we stood at Jack's door.

While we waited, I told Speechless about an idea that had been developing in the back of my brain.

'You know the Doc?' I said, to kick this off.

'Yes.'

'And Mr Soldoni?'

'Yeah, heard of him too.'

'Well, I've been thinking. You know your checklist

of things that might be linked? The bed and the equipment in the room under the chapel, tranced kids in or near the dungeons where the tunnel that leads to the chapel is, the idea that they might have been taken there and something done to them?'

'Yes.'

'And remember how Robbie and Ridley had itchy arms? Cat was holding her arm too out there.'

'Yes, where you pinched her.'

'Where I pinched her. But maybe the pinch hit the very spot something was put into her arm.'

'Put into it?'

'A needle, or needles, like you thought.'

'What are you getting at, Dax?'

'I'm getting at Withering and Soldoni constantly returning to the chapel—'

'Twice isn't constantly.'

'Twice is all we know about. Why would they be there even twice if they didn't have a reason to go there?'

'You tell me.'

'The room beneath the chapel.'

'You think they know about it?'

'More than know about it. The bed and equipment aren't ornaments. Someone's using them. Maybe two someones, working together.'

'You're thinking the students are being experimented on by Dr Withering and Mr Soldoni, the Head and Deputy Head?'

'Maybe they're not just the Head and Deputy Head,' I said.

'I don't get you.'

'Maybe they have a secret agenda, which involves experimenting on kids with the Lomas Gene.'

'I can't believe Dr Withering would experiment on his own daughter,' Speechless said.

'Adopted daughter.'

'Adopted as a baby, which makes her as much like his biological daughter as any girl could be.'

'Well, I think he's up to something. I think they both are, as a team.'

'I think you're crazy.'

'Crazy or just taking my imagination for a walk, like you said?'

'A walk, I said, not a mad run with its arms in the air.'

'Yeah, but what if they are doing stuff? Shouldn't we tell someone?'

'You mean the fuzz?'

'No, not the fuzz. Someone on the staff.'

'We can't do that. Tell this to any of the teachers and they'll go straight to Withering and Soldoni and we'll be out of here.'

'And the downside to that is...?'

'The downside,' he said, 'is that I've kind of got used to the place. That I would rather be here than back at the orphanage.'

'Anyway,' I said, 'I'm thinking Jack. He's not a teacher, and I'm sure he wouldn't go to the Head if we asked him not to.'

He looked doubtful. 'I'm not sure we should tell any adult something like this.'

'Oh, so we hang back while more kids get tranced and who-knows-what-else, do we?'

'I just think we should keep it to ourselves, for now at least.'

'Well I don't. So when they're done in there...'

When the door opened, Cat came out, all smiles, like nothing bad had happened in her entire life. Jack and Miss Piper stood behind her, also smiling.

The Doc and Mrs Withering immediately rushed to the scene and hugged Cat. I never expected to see the Doc hug anybody, dried up old stick that he is. (He seemed quite emotional actually.) Then he and his wife led Cat away, arms round her, while she said, 'I don't know what all the fuss is about. Everything's fine, there's nothing wrong with me...'

17

'Did you get anything out of her?' I asked Jack.

'Out of her?'

'About what caused the...whatever it was?'

He shook his head. 'I didn't dare probe too deeply for fear of making her focus on it, which might traumatise her.'

When Miss Piper said she had some library stuff to attend to, I asked Jack if I could talk to him about something.

'Of course. Come in.'

'Don't do it, Dax,' Speechless said. 'You're just guessing.'

I ignored him, Jack didn't hear him, and Speechless wandered off.

'Deckchair or stool?' Jack asked when he'd closed the door behind us.

'I'll stand.'

'Mind if I take the weight off?'

'It's your weight.'

He settled himself into the deckchair and put

his hands behind his head. All he needed was his trousers rolled up to the knee and an icecream in his fist and he'd be all set for a day on the beach.

'Shoot,' he said.

I told him what I had to say, and as I got into it he took his hands from behind his head and pulled himself as upright as he could in a chair like that, and when I'd finished, he said, 'An underground tunnel from the cells?'

'Yeah, they used to cart dead bodies along it.'

'A room with a bed and scientific equipment under the old chapel?'

'Very simple scientific equipment. Nothing too clever by the look of it.'

'And you think the students found in a trancelike state have been there, been subjected to...?'

'I don't know. But something, definitely something.'

He hauled himself out of the deckchair and stood before me, looking much more serious than usual.

'You can't really believe that Dr Withering and Mr Soldoni are doing something they shouldn't,' he said.

'Starting to,' I said. 'Why would they keep going to a ruined chapel if they don't have business there?

There's nothing there. Nothing *above* ground.'

'Oh, but *those* gentlemen?'

'So you don't believe me,' I said.

'You have to admit it's a lot to take in, Dax.'

'I know. But come and look at the room. I left the door at this end of the tunnel unlocked. We could get to it that way.'

He didn't rush out eagerly. Didn't even move. Didn't quite meet my eye either.

'What?' I asked.

'Do you mind if I mull this over for a bit?'

I frowned. 'Mull it over, or go to the Head with it?'

'No, I don't mean go to the Head with it. You've told me this in confidence. I wouldn't betray your trust like that. All I'm saying is, give me a little time.'

'How much time?'

'Overnight should do it, one way or the other.'

'What does one way or the other mean?'

'It means that I'll either think you're on to something or not be able to accept it.'

I sighed, nodded, muttered something like 'Right, OK, thanks,' and left the room.

I wandered to the lobby, disappointed that no one believed me right off, wondering if they were right not to, if maybe I was overthinking things, that the Doc and Mr Soldoni might not be up to anything...

Distant voices from outside.

I went to the front door. Across the courtyard, just the other side of the gateless gateposts, some of the students who'd gone in search of the missing hikers were gathering.

'Wonder if they've found that couple?'

Speechless had come up behind me. Then Dr and Mrs Withering and Cat were there too, and seconds later Miss Niffenegger and Mrs Page-Turner.

'They sound chirpy,' Miss Niffenegger said.

We all went down the steps and across the courtyard. At the gateless gateposts we found Mr Gladhusband's group. The other groups were returning too, and the cop car was tootling towards us along the road.

When the car stopped, the same policeman and policewoman got out. They looked less intense than before, and when the Doc introduced himself they broke into broad grins.

'Your pupils are a credit to you, Dr Withering,' the policeman said.

'Why, what have they done?' he asked.

'They've only found our missing couple, that's all.'

'So soon?' the Doc said. He looked a bit anxious when he said this.

'Yes! In no time at all.' This was the policewoman. 'Amazing!'

'Was it a particular group that found them?'

'Yes, that lady's.'

She pointed at Ms Samson, jogging after the bunch of kids who'd gone with her, which included Saxon

Tull, looking more full of himself than ever.

The cops thanked Withering like it was him who'd saved the hikers, turned their car around, and drove back along the road. Then the Doc asked Ms Samson what happened out there...

The couple the four groups had gone to look for were a pair of recently retired estate agents who'd come to Scrag Moor to get in some trekking in big boots after years looking round other people's homes, sitting behind desks, and talking on phones. They'd been well away from civilisation (easy on the moor, 'cos there isn't any) when it started to rain. They sheltered among some overhanging rocks, but then the rain got really heavy and came slanting in, and when they saw a little cave nearby they ran to it. While waiting in the cave for the rain to stop the man went further in, to look around. It was dark in the back of the cave and he didn't have a torch and failed to see where the ground had fallen in, and he fell after it (with a yell) and twisted his ankle when he hit the bottom (probably with an 'Ow!'). Hearing the yell, his partner went looking for him, but she also didn't have a torch and fell down after him. She was lucky she didn't twist something too, but that was because she landed on him. They tried shouting for help, but there was no one close enough to hear. They tried their phones too, but there was no signal. They were stuck down there for over two days – until Ms Samson's group found them.

It was Miyoko who located them, Miyoko Tanaka, whose power is sensing body heat, even through solid objects. She'd had it a few days and only used it for fun so far. With eight other kids in her group, plus Ms Samson, there was a lot of body heat around her, so Miyoko had deliberately separated herself from them and wasn't even looking in their direction when she thought she sensed the heat of two forms some way ahead, under the ground. She didn't call the others in case the forms weren't human, and wandered even further away –

'Miyoko! Please don't go off on your own!' Ms Samson bawled.

– until she came to the little cave the couple had sheltered in. She called into it and two voices answered from somewhere below. Then she called the others. The policeman and policewoman weren't near, so Ms Samson asked a couple from her group to run to where she thought they were and bring them. Then she asked the ones that had powers to think of ways to use them to get the couple out. Tilda Riddick, who can make suckers appear on her hands, offered to go down and see if there was an easy way to bring them up. Someone lent her a little torch, which she clenched between her teeth, and climbed down, sucker by sucker, head first, upside down. (I'm not sure why she didn't go down feet first. Maybe it felt more heroic the other way, sort of Spiderman-ish.) As the only light was the torch in Tilda's teeth, the couple couldn't see how she was coming, which was probably just as well. Tilda asked if they were hurt and the couple said not badly, and she climbed up again.

It was Billy Parker who came up with the next idea: to make his arms as long as he could (that's Billy's power) and grip the couple's hands so the others could pull him and them up. He folded himself over the side from the waist, and stretched his arms as far as they would go – about four metres – which turned out not to be enough, so he had to be lowered further down, with people holding his ankles. Billy gripped the woman's raised hands, but the combined strength of the people on his ankles wasn't sufficient to pull both him and her up. There was someone else there to solve that problem, though. Someone with super strength. That big-head Saxon Tull. Tull made his muscles grow, grabbed Billy's ankles, and hauled him and the woman up without any trouble. Then he did the same for the man.

They were all sitting or standing on the surface, away from the cave, when the police turned up. The hikers babbled on and on about how they'd been rescued – crazy stuff that the cops put down to stress and lack of water.

19

When the cops had driven off, the Doc said 'Well done' to Ms Samson's group, then turned to the others. 'Well done all of you – not least for not giving our game away!' Then everyone streamed into the courtyard, where Mr Banner the miserable caretaker was sweeping the cobbles with a big broom. He glared at everyone like they were tramping over his best carpet, then hoisted his broom and stalked off in an 'I don't know why I bother' sort of way.

Some of the kids hung about for a while, reliving the big adventure on the moor, but the rest went in to get something to drink or eat or whatever. I was one of those who stayed, but not to relive anything. I just wanted to be on my own. I wandered over to the side where the staff transport was parked. There were five cars plus Jack's Harley. Four of the cars were very ordinary. The fifth was Miss Piper's and it was small, and bright yellow, and covered with stick-on flowers. The kind of car to make you laugh just to look at it. I thought of her and Jack. Every adult in the school except Dr Withering and Mr Banner was nice and friendly in his or her way, but those two were the friendliest of all. They weren't teachers, of course, which could have been why you felt you could relax with them, say what you wanted. But Jack hadn't rushed to believe me about Withering and Soldoni, and I felt pretty let down by that. Wondered if I should have told Miss Piper instead. But then I thought, well, it was quite a thing to take in. Could be that if you're an adult you need time to get your head round such big deal stuff. Maybe tomorrow, when he'd got used to the idea, Jack—

'I want words with you, Daley.'

I turned. It was Cat, approaching with Speechless. The happy smile on her face when she left Jack's office was nowhere near it now.

'Speechless tells me that you think my father is some sort of master criminal,' she said.

'Remind me never to share my private thoughts with you,' I said to Speechless.

'It just came out,' he said, in my head as always.

'You really think,' Cat said, 'that my father would abduct his own students and...well, what do you think he's been up to?'

'I don't know,' I said. 'But something. Probably. And not just him.'

'Yes, I heard. Mr Soldoni too. First paintings that move, now this. You're not right in the head, Dax Daley.'

'OK.'

'OK? Is that all you've got to say?'

'Yep.'

I walked away.

'I haven't finished with you yet!' Cat shouted after me.

I shrugged, and carried on, out through the gateless gateposts once again.

There was no one else there now. I leant against the wall staring across the empty moor, not sure what to think about anything except that maybe I should give up thinking altogether. But even as that started to sound like a very good idea a tiny extra thought snuck in. The tiny extra thought went like this. The 'They shall not return' slab was in what remained of the old chapel. So was the wall full of painted people. Well. What if it wasn't the Doc and Mr Soldoni who were behind the trancing of the students? What if it was the people on the wall? This immediately brought another thought. The latest thought was: 'What sort of dummy are you, Daley? How could painted people put kids in a trance?'

Then a third thought started, but before it could shape itself into something that sounded like sense, a sharp squawk overhead made it shrivel back where it came from. I looked up. A big bird was soaring across the sky on wide wings, a smaller bird in its beak. I watched them go, almost envying the smaller bird. No worries for it about painted and unpainted people doing bad things. No worries about anything except 'How am I going to get out of this rotten beak?' Lucky little bird, I thought. Such a simple life. Any more big birds up there? Come and take me away too, big birds. Give me just one thing to think about. One small thing.

★

Byron was spending a second night in the cupboard under the stairs, but this time, to make sure he could get out without help, he left the door not quite closed. With him not using his bunk, Marcus had decided to have a sleepover with Howley Marsh, which meant I could have his bunk for the night. Nice change from the floor, though naturally I used my own pillow and duvet.

'Why would anyone in anything even close to his right mind,' I said to Speechless, 'want to sleep over in a cell identical to this, just three doors along?'

'He says he has a lot in common with Howley,' Speechless said.

'Dunno what,' I said. 'Marcus's power is flying and Howley's is invisibility. So what happens? Marcus wakes up in the night, turns the light on 'cos he fancies a chat, sees that Howley's not there and flies round the cell looking for him?'

'I don't care what they do as long as you don't do a Robbie Strogatz.'

'What do you mean?'

'Turn to water and wet the bed. You might drip, and wet mine too.'

'You can take the top bunk if you want,' I said.

'Oh yes. Then you get Saxon's muscles in your sleep and punch me in the back. No, I'll chance it where I am.'

I waited until we'd settled into our bunks with the lights off to tell him I had a couple of new theories about Withering and Soldoni.

'Two more theories?' he said wearily.

'Yes. The first concerns the painted wall in the old chapel. I've heard groans from that wall, but not any others. Why do you think that is?'

'I have no idea.'

'Because there are people on it. Actual groaning people.'

'Actual painted groaning people,' he said.

'Still people. So I'm thinking that Withering and Soldoni must have seen them move, and they know the people want to peel off the wall and take proper human form, but they can't do that without help. And the help is...a collection of Lomas Genes.'

'How would Lomas Genes bring painted people to life?' he asked.

'There's a lot of power in them. Who knows what they can do?'

'All right. But why would anyone want to help painted people come to life?'

'I don't know. Theory two.'

He yawned. 'Tell me in the morning.'

'Theory two. What if Withering and Soldoni are looking ahead?'

'Looking ahead?'

'Way ahead, to after we leave this dump. When we're sixteen or older.'

'What happens then?'

'They activate us.'

'Activate us? Dax, it's been a long day, and it's not getting any shorter.'

'They put us in a trance,' I said. 'All of us, one after

151

the other, and take us to the room under the chapel, implant some sort of tracking device in our arms so they'll know where we are in future, put things in our minds too, words or phrases that when they say them to us – over the phone, in a text or whatever – will make us use our powers to break into banks, or blow up buildings, or...something.'

'Nnnngggggnnnnggnnnngggg,' said Speechless.

I looked over the side of the bunk. 'What?' I asked.

'Nnnngggggnnnnggnnnngggg,' he repeated.

He was asleep. And snoring.

2

If ever a place was just perfect for bad dreams it was Scragmoor. And the dream I had that night was a doozy, and so vivid, like I was living every second of it, from the moment I started to roll off my mattress, realised just in time that I wasn't on the floor, and climbed down the little ladder instead.

It wasn't that I needed to go anywhere, it was just something I found myself doing. Had to do. I put my slippers on, my dressing gown, opened the door, went out. I didn't turn right and go to the bathroom, like I usually do if I wake in the night, but left, past the rest of the bedcells, and down the stairs to the lobby – quietly, so I wouldn't wake anyone. But I did wake someone. As I got to the foot of the stairs the cupboard under them opened and Byron scowled at me. 'Dax,' he said, 'if you have to come downstairs at night would you mind not doing it in hobnail boots?', and shut the door – tight.

I went from there to the Infirmary. Then to the door to the dungeons. I opened the door, turned the light on, went down the old stone stairs. There was no one else there, just me and rows of cells with waxwork prisoners in them, lying down or sitting up or standing around looking suicidal. At any other time I would have been pretty spooked down there alone at night, but I felt nothing as I walked past the cells, round the corner, past more cells, to the door at the end.

The door to the underground tunnel.

It was closed, of course, but I reached for the handle, and as I reached I started to experience a worry, and hesitated, and as I hesitated I heard a sound some way behind me. I didn't turn, though. I didn't look back. I couldn't. All I knew was that I had to go into the tunnel. I turned the handle. Pushed the door back. There was no light the other side. Nothing at all but total, endless blackness. But there was something. Something tall. Waiting for me.

I took a forward step.

Just one step. Then froze.

I froze because I could hear boots scraping the stone floor ahead of me, and gruff voices cursing, and a laugh from one of them, and then...there were men carrying boards with bodies on them, dead bodies, corpses, along the black tunnel, towards the room at the end.

All this filled my head as I stood with one foot inside the doorway, and as I stood there, listening to the men and watching them carry the bodies away, it came to me that I was about to go the same way as the dead, to the room, and up the stairs to the chapel, then outside, to an oblong Dax-sized hole with a small stone at the head of it.

A stone with my name on it.

This thought brought such horror that the body-carriers returned to the darkness, and the tunnel fell silent again, and all that was left was the tall figure that I couldn't quite make out, waiting for me to go on.

I would have done too – I didn't know how not to – if an arm hadn't looped round my neck from behind and pulled me back, out of the tunnel, and down, over my heels, onto the puller, hitting the ground a second after he scrambled out from beneath me. Then he leapt up and yanked the door shut, and tugged me to my feet, and back the way I'd come, round the corner, to the stairs. He pushed me all the way to the top and closed the door behind us and led me to one of the tables, sat me down, sat down opposite me, waited for me to collect my senses.

'What was all that?' I asked.

'You tell me,' said Speechless.

'I was dreaming. I think.'

'Dreaming you were going down to the dungeons and into the tunnel?'

'There was someone there,' I said.

'I didn't see anyone.'

'A dark shape. I couldn't make out his face. But I knew that he wanted me to come in. There were others too. Men with bodies. Carrying them, I mean.'

'I didn't see any men carrying bodies either,' he said. 'So maybe you really were dreaming. Sleepwalking, like Ridley was.'

'Two of us sleepwalking down there so soon after one another?'

'What else could it be?'

'Can we get out of here?' I asked.

'Back to the bedcell?'

'Somewhere that isn't a cell would be better right now.'

'How about the TV lounge? Watch a DVD to take your mind off this.'

'We're not supposed to watch DVDs after hours.'

'We'll keep the volume down.'

We crept to the TV lounge and closed the door super quietly. There's a cupboard in there with a lock on it, but it's an old lock, easy to open even without a key. Speechless rummaged in the cupboard, found a DVD, and stuck it in the player. I laughed when I saw the box.

'What's that doing here?'

'No idea, but if anything's an antidote to a bad bit of sleepwalking it's this.'

So we settled down to watch an episode of *In the Night Garden*.

We dozed off without kissing one another goodnight.

21

Now here's where we came in. The scene I mentioned at the start of all this.

The Infirmary, a few hours later. Sunday, breakfast time. Everyone seemed to be there but Byron. I checked the cupboard under the stairs but he wasn't there either. I didn't blame him for not wanting to eat with the rest of us. If he could hear everything ultra loud with just a few of us around, he would have been deafened by forty kids eating and talking and laughing and shouting in the same room. There was excitement from Nola Halloran, who'd woken with the ability to make inanimate objects speak, and dismay from Mandy Parr, who was covered in green scales that weren't there yesterday. One boy seemed kind of out of it today. Stephen Rimmer, the kid who could send objects flying just by thinking about it. He was sitting by himself, over in the corner, staring at an empty plate like he was wondering who'd swiped his grub.

Cat didn't join me and Speechless. She glanced

our way once and made sure I was looking before turning her back to show she was still cheesed with me.

'She's really taking it to heart, isn't she?' I said to Speechless.

'What, you calling her dad an arch villain?' he said. 'Yeah, such a little thing to get in a fricassee about.'

'Fricassee?'

'French stew.'

'Speechless, what are you on about?'

'I don't know. Must be the sleep deprivation.'

'You didn't have to follow me down there,' I said.

'Just as well I did, or who knows what would have happened to you.'

'It was just a dream,' I said.

'You really believe that, do you?' he said.

'Well...don't you?'

'I've been thinking about it, and the answer's no, I don't think you were dreaming. I think you were in a trance.'

'A trance? Me? Like the others?'

'Yes, you, like the others.'

'If I was in a trance, how come I can remember everything? No one else could.'

He shrugged. 'Maybe if you'd gone all the way along the tunnel to the room at the end your memory would have been wiped.'

'It might not have been. I might still remember everything. Then we'd know what happened to the others, and what to do about it.'

'Oh,' he said. 'So I didn't do you a favour, pulling you out of there?'

'That's not what I mean. Not exactly.'

'Not exactly, but close enough, eh? Right. Next time I won't interfere. Next time you're on your own.'

As we had no tremendously exciting plans for our day of rest, we were in no hurry to finish breakfast. The girls with the new powers made themselves scarce sooner than most – Nola to see if she could get the cars in the courtyard to talk to her, Mandy (the girl with the scales) to hide herself away in case her power turned out to be slithering across floors like a snake. Mandy had a fear of snakes. Well, a horror really. She hadn't gone near Diane Bentley since Diane got snakes for hair.

By the time we got up to go, there were only a few others left – Rendell Bude, Damian Lee, Scarlett O'Mara, Tilda Riddick, a couple more – and Stephen Rimmer, who still hadn't taken his eyes off his empty plate. But as we stood up Stephen lifted his head and looked at me, and then it was like he only had eyes for me instead of the plate. I thought of asking what he was staring at, but gave it a miss and started towards the door with Speechless. We'd taken no more than three or four steps when there was this clattering sound and all the knives, used and unused, lifted up from every table in the room, all by themselves. Just the knives, no other cutlery. Looking around, there seemed to be about thirty, all hovering at head height. Then we heard another clattery sound, from the serving counter this time, and more knives – much sharper ones – also lifted up and hovered in the air.

'That isn't normal,' I said to Speechless.

'Not very,' he said. 'And have you noticed where they're suddenly pointing?'

He said this because the knives, which had been pointing every whichway, had all turned, slowly, like they were drawn by a magnet, until every one was aimed at the only two people on their feet.

Him and me.

'I don't like the look of this,' I said – and realised I was talking to myself. Speechless had dropped to the floor and scurried under a table.

Now the knives were pointing at me alone.

I thought I would run a little test. The knives hadn't repointed at Speechless when he dropped below the angle they seemed comfortable being at. So maybe they would stay where they were if I moved too. I bent my knees, which took me about ten centimetres lower. And the knives – every single one of them –

dipped, so that they were still pointing at me.

At my head.

Now I really didn't like the look of this.

I stood up straight again, with a prickly feeling in the spine area. Also the heart, lungs, liver and kidney areas. I swallowed hard and took a single slow step forward. A slow long step.

The knives moved with me.

The room was utterly silent. You'd think someone would have had the decency to scream, wouldn't you? No one did. Probably because the knives were pointing at me, not them. I might have screamed myself to show them how it was done, but my throat had gone so dry it felt like a sack of sawdust.

I heard a scrape. Then more scrapes. Chairs. Two of the girls and three of the boys getting up and edging towards the door, bent almost double. Rendell and Damian were also standing now, though Damian was dropping slowly into a crouch that would take him below the knives and Rendell was reaching for the back of a chair.

Stephen Rimmer hadn't moved. He was still staring at me like I was a planet he'd always wanted to visit.

I was looking his way when he blinked half a dozen times in quick succession, and when he did that I heard a sharp fluttery sort of sound all around me.

And then the knives came. All of them at once.

Towards me.

Came so fast, from all sides, that I didn't have a hope of ducking in time, or even thinking about ducking. I just stood there while the end – a very bloody, messy end – zoomed my way.

But then, with less than half a second left for the highlights of my life to flash before my eyes – eyes that would soon have knives sticking out of them – there was a loud thudding and clattering sound as the knives hit something and dropped to the ground.

Then all was silent.

Silent and completely still.

I was unharmed, still standing, thirty or forty knives on the floor all round me, with Rendell at my side, holding the chair he'd leapt forward with to bat them away with his super speed.

No one moved for a very long moment. No one said a word or even made a sound – until someone started crying.

Stephen Rimmer.

'What's going on in here?' a voice said. 'Has something...?'

Mr Soldoni had breezed in, and skidded to a halt when he saw all the knives on the floor. Someone explained what little they knew.

'Knives?' Mr Soldoni said. 'Flying? By themselves?'

It was Stephen, of course. It turned out that he had no memory of anything since just before he came in for breakfast. A couple of others said they'd seen him collect a plate from the counter but not put anything on it, and take it to an empty table, and just sit there. He'd stayed like that until me and Speechless stood up, then he blinked, and the knives started flying. It wasn't until Rendell rushed forward and batted all the knives away with the chair that he came out of the trance he'd been in since before breakfast and realised that he was the one that had made them lift and fly at my head.

22

'They're trying to kill me,' I said to Speechless.

We were leaning against the wall of the old stables in the courtyard.

'You don't know that,' he said.

'All right, how would you put it?'

He thought about it, then nodded. 'They're trying to kill you. Someone is anyway.'

'But why?'

'Maybe it's your personality,' he said.

'No. It must be because I'm onto them.'

'Onto...?'

'Withering and Soldoni.'

'It might not be them.'

'Well, they're my prime suspects. My only suspects.'

I'd had a fit of the shakes about a minute after we left the Infirmary. Real honest-to-google, head-to-toe shakes. Mrs Withering happened to be near when they started and she rushed me to her room and sat me down, gave me water, said calming things till I hauled myself together. I was still a bit twitchy afterwards, though, outside with Speechless. Well, wouldn't you be? I mean how often are several handfuls of knives thrown at your head, point first?

'We have company,' Speechless said.

The company was Rendell and Cat.

'I just heard,' Cat said as they approached. 'What happened exactly?'

'If you've heard, you already know,' I said.

'Stephen Rimmer threw knives at you?'

'It wasn't Stephen. Well, it was, but he couldn't help himself.'

'Couldn't help throwing knives at you?'

'He didn't actually throw them. Not with his hands. His mind, yes, but he wasn't in control of that.'

'You're suggesting that someone else made him do it?'

'Am I missing something here?' Rendell asked.

'Long story,' I said.

'Oh. I hate long stories.'

'I owe you, Rendell. Big time.'

'You do,' he said, and walked away with his hand in the air.

We watched him go, then Cat leant against the wall with us.

'You think it has something to do with that room you say is under the chapel?' she asked.

'I think it has everything to do with it,' I said. 'And the people who put you and the others in a trance.'

'And you,' said Speechless.

Cat stared at me. 'You? When were you in a trance?'

'Ah...it might not have been a trance.'

'It was,' said Speechless. 'Last night. Middle of.'

'And there they are, suspects one and two,' I said, as Dr Withering and Mr Soldoni came out the front door and started down the steps.

'You're not going to let this go, are you?' Cat said.

'Not when one of them came into the Infirmary right after Stephen's knife-throwing act, no.'

'That doesn't prove anything.'

'Maybe not, but anyone could have come in, and it was one of them.'

'Which one?'

'Mr Soldoni. But if they're in it together...'

'They're not in it together,' Cat said firmly. 'They're in nothing together.'

'Maybe your dad's been led astray,' said Speechless.

She rounded on him as fiercely as if he'd said she really ought to do something about her hair. 'What do you mean, led astray?'

He flinched. She's taller than him, and a lot more scary.

'By Mr Soldoni,' he said. 'Your dad might not know what he's got himself into. Just a thought,' he added, glancing away from her blazing eyes.

'Anyone care to bet where they're going?' I murmured as the two men strolled towards the gateless gateposts.

'Hey, why don't we go and ask them?' Cat said sarcastically.

'Maybe we should,' I said, pushing myself away from the wall. 'One thing I'm not going to do is stand here and give them another shot at murdering me.'

'If another student tries to kill you while Dad and Mr Soldoni are off the premises, it would prove they're not behind it.'

Walking backwards, I said, 'Seeing as they can programme people to hurl knives at me in their absence it would prove nothing.'

'But my dad can't even programme a DVD player!' said Cat.

'We're not talking DVD players,' I said.

I spun round and marched away, but they came after me, and were only just behind me when I reached the gateless gateposts. Leaning out, I saw my suspects walking – as expected – towards the ruined village. They walked with their heads bowed, hands behind backs, like they were having a heavy conversation about tweed or Queen Victoria.

'What's the plan?' Speechless asked me.

'Follow them,' I said. 'See what they do.'

'Whatever it is, it'll be perfectly innocent,' said Cat.

'If it is, we'll see it, and we can cross them off the list.'

'There's a list?'

'No, not yet. No need for one with only two suspects.'

The mist was thicker than ever today, covering most of what could usually be seen of the moor from there. The nearer tors stood out like cardboard cutouts against a white wall.

'Let's get behind one of the tors in case they turn round,' I said. 'Then we can go after them tor by tor.'

'And afterwards we could say we tore along,' said Speechless.

I scowled at him. 'I won't even dignify that with a response,' I said.

He grinned. 'You just did.'

When we reached the nearest tor and went round the back of it we got quite a shock. There was someone there. Jack Toliver. He was just as startled to see us, but stepped quickly forward like he wanted to hide something – which made Cat instantly curious.

'What? Playing with dolls, at your age?'

'I just came across it,' Jack said. He sounded kind of embarrassed. 'I was taking a walk, and...'

Speechless was the next to look. He laughed.

'It's the image of Mr Banner!'

'Mr Banner the caretaker?' I said, and also looked.

There, standing at the base of the rock, was a brown-coated figure no more than twenty centimetres high that looked exactly like Mr Banner.

'Who would make a doll of that miserable man?' I chuckled.

Just then the little figure raised a hand. I jumped back. So did Cat and Speechless.

'It moves!' cried Speechless.

'It more than moves,' said Jack. 'It appears to be alive.'

I gaped from little Mr Banner to him. 'You heard Speechless?' I said.

He frowned. Then looked stunned. Then amazed.

'I did, didn't I?'

Him being the second adult to tune in to Speechless wasn't the biggest deal here, though. No, the biggest deal was the smallest. The Mr Banner doll wasn't just moving now, it was talking. Shouting actually, though its voice was too tiny for us to make out the words.

'It can't be the real Mr Banner,' said Cat. 'Can it?'

'I was wondering that very thing when you three strolled up,' said Jack.

'I think it is,' I said, leaning over the doll-like figure.

'But...how?' Cat said.

'Maybe one of the students suddenly got the power to shrink things and tried it out on him,' said Speechless.

'I like him better like this,' I said, eyeing the little man, who was still shouting – and pointing at Jack now, probably trying to get his attention. Jack couldn't make out what he was shouting any more than we could.

'What if he can't be brought back to his full size?' Cat said.

'Then he'll need a special house,' said Speechless.

'There's a dolls' house in the old stables,' I said.

Mr Banner must have heard this because he stopped shouting and sank to the ground looking even less happy than usual, which you wouldn't have thought possible.

'We should take him back to the school,' Cat said. 'He'll be safer there. Less risk of his being carried off by crows or whatever.'

'Or eaten by foxes,' said Speechless.

'Stabbed by passing hedgehogs,' I said.

Little Mr Banner put his head in his hands and sobbed.

'I vote that Dax takes him,' said Cat.

'You want me gone because of what I think your dad's been up to,' I said.

'Still suspicious of Dr Withering and Mr Soldoni, Dax?' Jack asked.

'Oh, he's told you, has he?' said Cat. 'Yes, he is. But I know my dad's not doing anything bad. Or Mr Soldoni. I just want it proved, so he'll shut up about it.' She paused. 'You wouldn't ask them, would you?'

'Ask them?' Jack said. 'Ask Dr Withering and Mr Soldoni if they're up to no good?'

'Yes. It would probably sound better coming from an adult.'

He gave an uncomfortable half laugh. 'I'm not sure a question like that would sound right coming from anyone, actually.'

'Please?' she said, all big-eyed and pleading.

'But I don't even know what they're suspected of,' Jack said. 'Not exactly.'

'Tell them your latest theories,' Speechless said to me.

'Theories?' said Cat. 'He has two more?'

'Oh yes. One's about your dad and Mr Soldoni trying to bring the painted people in the chapel to life.'

Cat gaped at me. 'You think that?'

'The other one's even better,' Speechless said. 'Tell them about the implanted words and phrases and tracking devices, Dax.'

'Tracking devices?' gasped Cat.

I glared at Speechless. 'I thought you were asleep when I told you that.'

'It was late, I didn't want to hear it. Go on, tell them. All three of them.'

23

So I told them. But said out loud in the misty light of day to a full-grown adult and a doll-sized one, it sounded crazy even to me.

'Now that's what I call a theory!' Jack said warmly when I was done.

Cat was less complimentary. 'Rob banks?' She sneered. 'Blow up buildings?'

'Just a wild thought,' I said lamely.

Jack chuckled. 'Oh, it's wild all right. But it's given me an even wilder one. What if the guilty parties are harvesting the essence of the Lomas Gene? Extracting samples from several copies of it to distil into a potion to give themselves powers.'

'A potion?' said Speechless. 'To drink?'

'Yes, to drink.'

'Give themselves powers?' said Cat. 'Powers plural? More than one?'

'Why not? It's believed that every copy of the Gene provides one power. So for an individual to get more than one he'd need access to additional versions of it. Imagine if one person possessed a whole stack of powers. Be hard to ignore someone like that for long, wouldn't it?'

'Dax has a stack of powers, and we can ignore him,' Cat said.

Jack looked startled. 'More than one power? Dax?'

I scowled at Cat. 'Thanks a lot – friend.'

She sniffed haughtily and looked away. 'Ex friend.'

'I didn't know you had even one,' Jack said to me. 'But you have more than one power?'

'They're not my powers,' I said. 'Not really. I kind of...borrow them.'

'Borrow them? Sorry, I...?'

I sighed, but explained.

'So you don't have one *specific* power,' Jack said when I'd finished.

'No. Be a lot simpler if I did. And they come and go when they feel like it, which doesn't help. Now do you mind if we change the subject and never mention it again this side of eternity?'

'Of course,' Jack said. 'But Dax.'

'What?'

'That's quite a thing you have there.'

'Yeah. Right. Subject change?'

'OK. How about this one? If two people were somehow extracting Essence of Lomas Gene, wouldn't one of them have to know quite a bit about genetics, and that particular top-secret gene in particular?'

We agreed that he would.

'And who do you suppose would know more about it than anyone else?'

'The person who discovered it?' Cat suggested.

'Precisely.'

'I think we'd have heard if Reinhardt Lomas was here,' said Speechless.

'I'm sure you would,' Jack said. But he smiled as he said it.

'You mean he might be here, pretending to be someone else, using a different name?' said Cat.

Jack spread his hands and left it to us to think it through.

'Soldoni sounds like a made-up name,' I said.

Jack's smile broadened, like I'd really hit the nail.

'You're not seriously suggesting that Mr Soldoni is a top genetic scientist passing himself off as

Deputy Head in order to get to the gene he discovered and he's persuaded my father to help him?' Cat said to Jack.

'It wasn't me who pointed the finger at Mr Soldoni,' Jack reminded her.

She flipped to me. 'Is that what you're suggesting?'

I held my hands up, palms out. 'I'm saying nothing.'

'He could be one of the others,' said Speechless.

Now we all looked at him.

'I mean Lomas might not be Mr Soldoni. He might be another member of staff, keeping his head so far down that we haven't even begun to suspect him yet.'

'He'd have to have an accent with a name like that,' I said.

'Not necessarily. We don't know where he was born.'

'Well, if he was here and pretending to be someone,' said Cat, 'my money would be on one of the male super tutors.'

Jack gave a hoot of laughter. 'Mr Gladhusband or Mr Cosmo a renowned geneticist turned evil genius? That's the funniest thing I've heard in all the time I've been here.'

'Even if someone else is behind the trancing,' I said, 'we need to rule out Cat's dad and Mr Soldoni first.'

'I don't,' Cat muttered.

I asked Jack if he'd thought over what I said about them yesterday.

'Actually, that was my reason for coming out here,' he said. 'Needed to get away from the school to try and get it right in my head.'

182

'And did you manage it?'

'Mr Banner came along before I'd got that far. Then you three.'

'So you still don't believe me.'

'Still at the open mind stage, Dax.'

'OK. But while it's still open would you mind seeing what you can get out of them? They're over in the ruined village' – I glanced at Cat – 'again.'

Jack looked a bit uneasy about this, but after thinking it over, said, 'It might help if you were there too. All of you. Then I could say we were chatting and strolling nearby, and we saw them, and...well, play the rest by ear.'

'Let's do it,' I said.

'We can't leave Mr Banner,' said Cat.

I'd forgotten Mr Banner. We all had. He was still sitting on the ground, still looking like the unhappiest doll you ever saw.

'We can't take him with us,' Cat said. 'But we must make sure he's safe while we're away.'

She gathered some small stones and built a wall round him. While she was doing this, little Mr Banner glared at her like she was building his very own doll-sized prison cell.

'Don't worry,' Cat assured him. 'We'll return very soon and take you back. Till we do, keep your little head down, eh?'

24

The Season of Mists was really living up to its name today, especially around the village. It was like a bunch of ghost ruins. You could easily imagine grey zombies in rags coming out of them, shuffling slowly towards you, catching you as you tried to do a high-speed sprint away.

When we got to the outer wall of the chapel we gathered behind it, with Speechless (the shortest) doing the peering-round-the-corner thing.

'See them?' I asked him.

'No, not y... Oh, there they are. They're coming out of one of the cottages and heading our way.'

'Our way?'

'Towards the chapel, which is just the other side of this wall, so keep the chat down. They might not be able to hear me, but they can you.'

So we stood there, listening silently. The Doc and Mr Soldoni were talking quietly, but we managed to make out most of what they said.

'It's been here since the Middle Ages.' This was Mr

Soldoni. 'It's part of Scragmoor's history.'

'And it's clearly at the end of its history,' replied the Doc. 'With so little left of it, there's nothing to adapt for other uses. We have to make up our minds, Jim. We're spending more time here than at the school.'

'I know, I know, but...'

Silence for a minute, then Mr Soldoni said something else.

'And what about this tomb, or whatever it is? If we remove the rest of the roof and the outer wall, it'll be completely exposed.'

'No more than the graves outside,' said Withering.

I took a turn to look round the wall. They stood looking down at the 'They Shall Not Return' slab.

'Could be an entire family under here,' Mr Soldoni said.

'If there is, it's a long-forgotten one,' answered the Doc. 'There's not even a name to commemorate them. We can't afford to be sentimental about people no one remembers or will miss.'

'They know nothing about it!' Speechless said, in every head except the two in the chapel.

A finger and thumb pinched my neck – hard. I

only just managed not to squeal. I looked over my shoulder, at Cat, mouthing a single word at me.

'See?'

'All right, they're exonerated,' Jack whispered. 'But rather than sneak off and risk being seen I think I'd better have a word anyway. You stay here.'

He put a finger to his lips and went round the wall. Huddled together behind it, we heard the Doc's surprise at seeing him, then him and Mr Soldoni telling Jack that they'd been trying to decide for days what to do about the chapel, especially as the firm who'd been paid to make the buildings safe had gone out of business and weren't coming back.

And then...

....everything went quiet.

No more talk.

Utter silence.

We waited expectantly, but nothing else came. Not a word, not a sigh, not a burp. We were about to look round the wall to see if the three of them had gone somewhere else, when the Doc and Mr Soldoni walked out, and right by us. We looked at one another, puzzled. They must have seen us. Couldn't have missed us, standing there.

Cat ran after them, past them, stopped in front of them, spoke to them. They stepped round her and walked on like they didn't want to talk to her. She put her fists on her hips and yelled 'What have I done?' at their backs. They didn't stop, or pause, or turn, just carried on walking.

Cat came back to us.

'They ignored me,' she said. 'Totally ignored me. Both of them.'

'That's one power I'd like to have,' I said.

We went into the chapel. The people on the wall looked like they were trudging through fog. Even Jack, waiting for us, looked like he was growing out of the mist rolling across the floor. He knew what was bothering Cat before she said a thing.

'They didn't see or hear you,' he said. 'If you'd knelt down in front of them and they tripped over you, they would have got up and walked on as if nothing had happened.'

'How come?' Cat asked.

'I removed their awareness of your being here. All three of you. And me.'

'You hypnotised them?' I said.

'It seemed best to remove their memory of coming here today, and of us. Safer all round.'

'Handy, that,' said Speechless. 'Being able to edit memories.'

'Oh, that's nothing,' Jack said.

He pointed at a heap of brickwork on the ground – part of one of the walls that had caved in years ago. Something as bright as a bolt of lightning sprang from his finger and the bricks flew apart like they'd been struck by an enormous hammer.

25

We gaped. Of course we did.

'Power,' said Jack. 'Wonderful thing. You lot don't know how lucky you are.'

'I don't have a power,' said Cat, still gaping.

'Or me,' said Speechless.

'But you will, before long. And you, Dax, you appear to be uniquely blessed.'

I found my voice, which had taken a short break while my mind imploded. 'You pointed at that bit of wall,' I said, 'and...and...'

Jack pointed at another heap of fallen masonry, a second bolt of brightness shot from his finger, and that shattered too.

'How do you do that?' said Cat.

'I simply extend my finger and think what I want it to do,' he said.

'But that has to be a power. And Lomas Gene kids are the only ones who...'

She shook her head, understanding it as much as me and Speechless, which was not at all.

'The Lomas Gene has a very narrow activation window,' Jack said. 'It's believed that it'll last a lifetime once it's in place, but that a power can't kick in fully until the carrier is eleven or twelve, and that if it's not operational by the early teens it never will be.'

'So you have the Lomas Gene?' I said. 'You've had a power since you were eleven or twelve?'

He laughed. 'Me? No!'

'But...'

'Remember my crackbrained theory about someone distilling Gene samples garnered from Scragmoor students with a view to giving himself powers?'

'Yes...'

'Well guess what.'

He flicked a hand, and Speechless flew backwards, landing on the ground with a hearty 'Oof!'

Cat stared at Jack for a second, then ran to Speechless.

I stayed put. I don't think I could have moved a millimetre just then. But struck by a sudden thought, I said, 'Little Mr Banner. It wasn't you who...?'

Jack grinned. 'It was.'

'So that's why he was pointing at you and shouting. He was trying to tell us it was you who shrank him.'

'I had no idea I could do that until it happened,' he admitted. 'I'd actually gone there to decide what to do about you, Dax, when Mr Banner came by. He was having one of his usual grumbles, and suddenly he was at my feet, as shocked as I was. That left me with a further dilemma – how to dispose of him – when you three appeared.'

'Dispose of him?' said Cat, leading Speechless back to us. He was limping a bit, and holding his backside.

'I was coming round to the idea of a little crack on the head with a stone followed by a small hole in the ground covered in earth.'

'You'd have killed him?'

'Either that or removed the relevant bit of his memory, as I did with Dr Withering and Mr Soldoni just now. When we're done here I'll go back and do one or the other, if he hasn't already returned to his proper size and blown my cover.'

I couldn't believe what I was hearing. I just had to be getting it wrong.

'It isn't you who's been trancing the kids, is it?' I said.

192

He clapped his hands lightly. 'Well done, Dax.'

'But...but...'

'Yes, your theory about Dr Withering and Mr Soldoni, though very entertaining, was some way off the mark.'

'And it was you who kitted out that room? The bed, the equipment and so on?'

'Yes, in dribs and drabs, mostly during the week or so before the school opened.'

'Just to be clear,' said Speechless. 'You put four students in a trance, including Cat, and made some sort of concentrate from their Lomas Genes in a room below this chapel?'

'It's not quite as simple as that,' Jack said, 'but that's it in principle.'

'And you've got the same powers as those four? You can fly like Marcus, disappear like Ridley, turn to water like Robbie, see in the dark like Cat?'

'Seeing in the dark's not a power,' Cat snapped. 'How many more times?'

Whether it was a power or not, Jack was shaking his head.

'It doesn't work like that. The so-called Lomas Gene

is rare, but not restricted to the forty-one of you. In the beginning, powers thrown up by the Gene were expected to reflect the holder's background, class, ethnicity, character, and all manner of other things, so when offering places at Scragmoor, SH1 tried to create a varied mix, believing that diversity would deliver a variety of abilities.'

'If that's true,' said Cat, 'how come that right at the start of term three very different boys developed the power of invisibility?'

'It was a false assumption,' Jack said.

'Uh?'

'It's now understood that whatever's gone before in a Lomas Gene carrier's life, whatever kind of person he or she is, the Gene alone decides what power to give them. The type of power can't be predicted. There's no guarantee that even twins with the Gene would develop an identical power.'

'So you haven't got the same powers as Cat and the other three,' I said.

'No.'

'And all you can do is smash bits of wall and shrink people?'

'And throw them across chapels,' added Speechless.

Jack smiled tautly, but didn't answer.

'Why are you doing this?' Cat asked him. 'What do you hope to gain?'

'I'll tell you what I don't want,' he answered. 'To end up on a scrapheap like my old man. Thirty-two years in a factory, then kicked out thanks to cutbacks by the government he'd voted in. He never worked again and never got over what he saw as a betrayal.'

'In other words you want to be noticed.'

'I confess that the prospect does have some appeal.'

'But you must have been noticed doing your stage act – or was that a lie too, like everything else?'

'Oh, I had an act all right, and of course I was noticed – until the curtain came down. What I want is to keep the curtain up, permanently, and in order to do that I must cover my tracks by cutting the chances of the truth leaking out.'

'From us, you mean?' said Speechless.

'You're the only ones who know it,' Jack said.

'So what are you going to do, wipe our memories too?'

'Unfortunately, I can't be a hundred percent certain that one of you won't eventually remember something of what you've just learned and inform people who would try to thwart me.'

'Which means?' asked Cat.

'Which means,' Jack said, 'that you three must die today.'

26

'D-die?' said Speechless, the first to get his brain round such a complicated word.

'You'd kill us?' said Cat. 'You'd actually kill us?'

'Question of expediency, I'm afraid,' Jack said.

Cat's head swivelled on me with fury, like this was my fault.

'What do you have to say about your lousy theories and accusations now, Dax Daley?'

I had no answer to that.

'How would you...do it?' Speechless asked Jack.

'I'm thinking the roof.' He tilted his head to look up. 'The bit that's left is just begging to come down, and when it does I'll make a miraculous escape, appear bruised and battered and very tearful, and be lauded for my selfless but tragically inadequate efforts to save you.'

'You could really bring the roof down?'

'You saw what I did to the fallen masonry.'

'That was already on the ground.'

'I've been practising, out on the moor, riding

round demolishing abandoned old buildings with a finger, flick of the wrist, wave of the hand. I don't know why all the powers I have are in my hands, but I imagine that by sipping the essence of other Lomas Genes I'll acquire a wider variety before long. Then I'll have some real fun.'

'Last night...' I said.

He looked at me. 'Last night?'

'I woke up and went down to the dungeons – couldn't help myself – and I opened the door to the tunnel. Did you make me do that?'

'Naturally, who else?'

'Was it you I thought I saw waiting for me in there?'

'It was.'

'How did you make me go down there?'

'I planted a small command in your mind in my office yesterday, while you were telling me about your suspicions of the good doctor and Mr Soldoni.'

'A command? You can't have. I would have noticed.'

'Noticed me saying "Look into my eyes" in sonorous tones or waving a pocket watch like a pendulum until you lost awareness of what I was saying, you mean?'

'Well...yes.'

'There are various kinds of hypnosis, Dax. On you I used what's more often than not called conversational hypnosis.'

'What happens with that?'

'We chat, I distract you with an unrelated word or phrase that causes you to shift focus, and in the seconds that you're thinking about the distraction I slip a small suggestion into the dialogue. You've heard of sleight-of-hand? Think sleight-of-mouth.'

'And that's why I woke up last night and went down to the tunnel?'

'That's why.'

'If Dax was in a trance it didn't last,' said Speechless. 'He snapped out of it as soon as I pulled him back from the doorway.'

'It was a very slight one,' Jack said. 'He wouldn't have so easily come out of the one I would have put him into in the room below us if you'd left him to follow me there.'

'Where you planned to extract some of his Lomas Gene essence, I suppose,' said Cat.

'That and plant a deeper command which,

sometime this morning, would have made him climb to one of the loftiest, least safe parts of the old prison, where he would have slipped or missed his footing and fallen without complaint or sound to the ground far below.'

'But that would have been murder!' Cat said.

'No, it would have been an accident. I would have been nowhere near the scene when gravity claimed him.'

'Still murder.' She glared.

'It must have been you who made Stephen Rimmer throw knives at me then,' I said to Jack.

'Of course it was.'

'How?'

'Oh, just a little command popped into his subconscious as we exchanged a few words of greeting before breakfast. Very easily done.'

'Why did you want to kill me before we knew you were behind all this?'

'I didn't want to, Dax. It seemed wise, that's all. If I'd succeeded, these two would almost certainly have set aside the suspicions of skulduggery you were filling their heads with, and I could have continued to draw students to the room below while blaming the atmosphere and history of Scragmoor for their temporary confusion.'

'If that room's been set up since the start of term,' I said, 'how come you've only just started to put us in trances and extract this...essence?'

'It's a new procedure,' Jack said. 'There's no manual for it, so patience had to be exercised while it was fine-tuned. Rather frustrating for me, having to bide my time for so long. I like to get on with things.'

'Is your name really Jack Toliver?' Speechless asked suddenly.

Jack smiled. 'So many questions. Trying to delay the end, are we?'

'Is it, though?'

'Some weeks ago, I was on my way here, wondering how I could talk my way onto the staff – as a general handyman if need be – when I stopped off at a pub on the edge of the moor. There I fell into conversation with a nice young chap who told me his name was Jack Toliver, that he was heading for Scragmoor to take up his first ever position as a psychologist, and that he was hitching, as he wasn't yet a qualified driver. I kindly offered him a lift on the back of my Harley.'

'How far did he get?' Cat asked coldly.

'About half way. Poor fellow contracted a severe case of broken neck and fell down a crevasse.'

'And you took his place.'

'How could I not? A counsellor was expected, to steer the school's students through anticipated stormy waters. I couldn't let everyone down.'

'Your real name?' Speechless asked again.

'Bernard Marx, at your service.' Jack made a low, theatrical bow. 'And now,' he said, straightening up, 'do you mind if we get on with our little bit of business?'

'What's to stop us making a run for it?' Cat asked.

'I'm glad you asked that.'

He waggled his fingers at us, and at once we couldn't move or speak or even blink. We were as good as frozen, if not as cold.

'I have one more question,' Speechless said, in all our minds.

Jack laughed. 'There's no shutting you up, is there? Go on then, seeing as I'm in such an accommodating mood.'

'How do you extract genetic material and liquidise it?'

'Ah, well, I'm afraid that's out of my area of expertise. My part in this little enterprise is to put the students into a trance so the procedure can be carried out without their knowledge, then, some time afterwards, when they're well away from the scene of operations, remove any residual memory of it.'

'Your part in it? You mean you're not alone? It's not just you?'

'Oh no, it's not just me. I know nothing of genetics, or how to locate genes, let alone drain off some of their essence.'

'Then who?' Speechless said.

'Who? I told you back at the tor.'

'You didn't.'

'Oh, I did. But do you mind if we expedite this? Long-winded final scenes are so boring, I find.'

He raised his arms. But just as he did so there was a roar from one side of us, then roars from the other side, and a horde of horrible beasts with slavering jaws and terrible teeth rushed at us – all four of us – and reached for us like they wanted to tear us apart and spit out the gristle. The only one who could defend himself was Jack, who was flapping his hands wildly to ward off the creatures, but the attack must have cut the power he'd used to freeze us, because suddenly we could move again – not that it helped much, with the monsters roaring and shrieking all round us. I mean there wasn't enough leisure time to sit back and think, 'Hmm, I wonder who these beasties are and what they can be after?' But while covering my head to stop it being bitten off,

I glimpsed Speechless, standing there with his eyes shut, like there was nothing to be afraid of.

And I realised.

There were no monsters.

Speechless was putting them into our minds!

I was still looking at him when he started, opened his eyes like he'd sensed something, and the monsters vanished in puffs of mental smoke. He'd sensed something all right, and I saw what, and a second later Cat did too, but Jack didn't, because he wasn't facing the painted wall like we were. All he saw, with the monsters gone, was us, standing before him in a row.

'Which one of you did that?' he demanded.

'Not me,' I said.

'Did what?' said Cat.

'I had my eyes shut,' said Speechless.

The mist drifting across the wall made the painted people look kind of hazy, but not so hazy that you couldn't see them moving. All of them. Some looked like they'd just woken up. Stared around like they were trying to get a grip on where they were.

'It's true then,' Cat said in a hushed voice.

'Maybe next time you'll believe me,' I replied.

'Don't hold your breath,' she said.

27

If Jack noticed that we were looking at something behind him, he was too angry to show that he cared. He held his hands out towards us, palms up, raised them slowly, and we felt ourselves lifting off the ground. As it's not natural to lift off the ground unless there's something under you, we threw our arms out in a mini panic, and when we did that...

... Jack's feet also left the ground!

'Eh?' he said, looking down.

I glanced at the others. They seemed as surprised as him. Which meant...

'Um,' I said. 'I think that might be me.'

'You?' said Jack.

'Borrowing that one from you. Sorry, I can't help it.'

'Ah, the multi-powered Dax Daley at work,' he said. 'Well, Dax, copy this!'

And, still hovering, he thrust one hand in my direction, like he was pushing hard at something, and I flew backwards across the chapel, crashed against the only other standing wall, grunted (cos it hurt), and slithered down it.

Cat and Speechless were also back on the ground by this time, sprawling where they'd fallen, and Jack was down too, but on his feet. 'Now I really must finish this,' he said. 'So if you'll forgive me...'

Then the three of us were hauled together as though by some invisible rope, and bundled into a tight group. We could move, but couldn't pull apart or break away from each other. Not only that but we were standing directly below the section of roof Jack planned to bring down on us.

He stepped back, closer to the wall of painted people, turned his face up to the misty sky, and raised his arms, full stretch and spread wide like he was about to cry out to some old god. There was a lofty creak from way up high, and bits of plaster and wood trickled down onto our upturned faces.

'Ooh,' Speechless said suddenly. 'Did you hear that?'

'If you mean the roof getting ready to crush us,' I said, 'yes, thanks.'

'Not the roof. The people on the wall. They're groaning.'

I couldn't hear them this time, and Cat can't have either because she said, 'Since when did you have super hearing?'

'I don't think I'm hearing them,' he said. 'I'm picking them up in my head.'

'Oh, that old thing.'

Obviously Jack hadn't heard the groans either. He was still staring at the roof, like he was willing it to fall. Willing and willing and willing. And it was dipping now, dipping badly.

'Dax,' said Cat. 'All the powers you've borrowed or copied or whatever it is. Can't you do something useful with just one of them?'

'Like what?'

'Like get us out of this. A spot of teleportation would be quite welcome right now. Make us disappear and reappear somewhere else, well away from here, preferably with candyfloss in our fists and our feet in a paddling pool.'

'None of the students have got a power like that, so I can't borrow it,' I said. 'Also, I can't get the powers to work when I want.'

'You lifted Jack off the ground just now.'

209

'Yeah, but I didn't plan it. If you asked me to do it again I wouldn't know how.'

'Jack can work his powers when he wants to.'

'He's been practising, I haven't.'

'Why haven't you?'

'Because I don't want any powers. I spend most of my time trying to stop them working.'

'Dax,' Cat said. 'Concentrate. This is the moment you prove at last that there's some point to you. You fly up to the roof, hold it while Speechless and I escape, then let it fall and turn Jack into a smoothie. Then we stand around outside smiling and feeling good about ourselves to closing music and rolling credits.'

'You watch too much TV,' I said.

'Wish I was watching it now. That roof will be down in less than a minute.'

'That long, you think?'

'I'm trying to look on the bright side.'

'Ooh,' said Speechless again.

'Don't tell me,' I said. 'The wall people are starting to sing.'

'No, they've fallen silent. But look.'

We looked. And saw two of the painted people

210

reaching out of the mist. It was the same two as before, the meanest-looking of the men, and they were reaching for the nearest person who wasn't on the wall, which was Jack, whose back was to them. One hand of each man gripped Jack's shoulders from behind, and he brought his eyes down from the roof and looked from one hand on one shoulder to the other on the other. At the same time, he lowered his arms and we were no longer bound together. We separated, but not by much, and stood watching the painted men pull Jack backwards. He looked more puzzled than scared, but because they gripped him

so firmly he was unable to turn to see who they were.

'What's this, Dax?' he said. 'What are you playing at now?'

'Not me this time,' I said. 'Not any of us.'

Now, as the men pulled him closer and closer, others in the painting rearranged themselves to make room for an extra figure. Then Jack...I don't really know how to describe this, but...well, they pulled him into the wall.

Into the painting, with them.

'That woman,' said Speechless. 'Third from the end. She's saying something.'

'I can't hear her,' said Cat.

'What's she saying?' I asked.

'Hang on, I'll see if I can pass her words into your heads...'

And he did. And this is what we heard.

'*I didn't do it. I told them and told them. It was Colly burnt the neighbours' cottage down, not me. Colly killed the family, and they sent me to the gallows. He hanged me personally, for his own crime, smiling that hateful smile as he did it. Help me! Help me!*'

We couldn't help her, of course. Her bones had been

under the ground for a very long time, and all that was left of her was her painted image on the wall, along with those of others who'd dropped through the Hanging Shed floor way back – them plus one other.

Jack.

Who was now part of the painting.

'What do we do?' Cat said. 'How do we get him out of there?'

'We don't,' I said.

'But we can't leave him there.'

'We can. And that roof's not gonna stay up there much lon—'

I didn't finish. Didn't need to, because the roof was coming down, the entire mass of it, in what looked like slow motion, right over where we were standing. I glanced back at the painted wall. The people were looking up too – all except Jack, who was staring helplessly at us.

'I think we need to go,' said Speechless.

'I know we need to,' I said.

Then there was this long, slow, creaking sound, and a cracking, and a snapping, and a tumbling, a

213

rumbling, a slithering, and the roof was well and truly on its way to the last place we wanted it to be – us.

We ran.

Like stink.

We were about ten metres from the chapel and still running when a horrendous crash told us that the roof had made it to the floor. Turning at a safe distance we saw that it had taken with it most of the outer wall that we'd just run round. Dust leapt up from the new rubble and turned the white mist grey, but through it we could see that the back wall – and only the back wall – was still standing. No surprise really as it was part of the strong high wall that encircled the school. The painted figures were no longer moving, though. None of them. Like before, some looked mournful, some looked angry, some mean, and all of them were trudging nowhere. The only difference now was that there weren't eighteen of them any more.

There were nineteen.

28

We stood there for at least a minute watching the dust settle and waiting to see if Jack would move. He didn't. Even from that distance we could see a puzzled look on his face, which was half turned towards us, but he didn't even blink. He couldn't. He was part of the painting now.

'What I don't get,' I said, '*one* of the things I don't get, is why they all came to life this time.'

'Didn't they before?' Cat asked.

'No, just a couple of them, maybe three or four. The others looked like they might, but I didn't stick around to see.'

'Maybe you should have.'

'Oh yes, then you'd be standing here looking at me as part of the painting.'

'A painted Dax might have been an improvement on the live one.'

'My guess is the power of massed Lomas Genes,' Speechless said. 'Look how they affect Byron. And it's not the first time the Gene's brought something to life, is it?'* Us three being together at the chapel the first time might have caused the people in the painting to stir, but you were the only one to see it. And just now we were there again, plus Jack and the essence of the four Genes he'd swallowed. That's a lot of power.'

'Others have seen them move at this time of year,' I said, 'and they didn't have the Lomas Gene.'

'Yeah, but did they?' Speechless said.

* *Speechless means something that's described in* Eye of the Gargoyle *(Hero 41 Book One).*

216

'Did they what?'

'See them move. Or did they imagine it? The Scragmoor books in the library are full of legends and old tales, and the moor is a pretty atmospheric sort of place.'

'What *I* don't get,' said Cat, rubbing her arm where I pinched it earlier, 'is why they wanted to take a live person into the wall at all.'

'Maybe they reached for Jack because he was nearest, hoping he'd pull them out, but pulled him in, instead,' I suggested.

'That's ridiculous.'

'Of course it's ridiculous. This whole business is ridiculous. How often do you come across paintings that move and groan and speak and make living people part of them?'

'Is your arm still sore?' Speechless asked Cat.

'Yes. Feels like someone pinched me...'

'Let's see.'

'See what?'

'Your arm.'

'Why?'

'Because the others who were tranced and donated

Essence of Gene also had itchy arms, right where you do.'

She rolled up her sleeve and showed us the place she'd been rubbing: a red circle the size of a shirt button, surrounded by tiny dots like pinpricks.

'You think they extracted the essence through our arms?' she asked.

No one had a chance to answer this because just then there was a shout from up ahead, and some tutors and students were running towards us.

'What happened down there?' bellowed Mr Kanwar, leading the charge.

'The old chapel collapsed!' we bellowed back.

'You weren't in it, were you?'

'No! Course not! It's out of bounds!'

When he and the others ran past us to investigate, Cat said, 'We should go and see to little Mr Banner.'

We were half way to where we'd left him when the sun burst through the mist and Cat and I had to shield our eyes to see. Speechless didn't shield his because he was walking with his head down, looking thoughtful.

'Do you realise,' he said, 'I can make people think they're being attacked by nightmare creatures. My power must be expanding.'

'Oh, so you finally admit it *is* a power,' I said.

'I think it must be.'

He didn't sound nearly as down about this as he did previously.

'If it is,' I said, 'and you ever put monsters in my skull again, I'll show you what a *real* monster can do.'

Mr Banner was right where we'd left him, behind the tor on the far side of the road. But there was something different about him now. The something different was that he'd grown back to his proper size. He was sitting with his back against a boulder, eyes closed, snoring.

'Must have dozed off when he was little and grown back in his sleep,' Cat said.

'If he did, he'll probably think he dreamed it,' said Speechless.

'Well, we can stop worrying about him now,' I said. 'Leave him to wake up in his own time.'

We turned towards the school. We were almost there when we heard a toot behind us. We were on the opposite side of the road to the one the chapel was on, so when Miss Piper pulled up alongside us in her cheerful little car she wasn't looking in that direction. If she had been she couldn't have missed the collapsed building or the exposed back wall. She wore big sunglasses, and with her cool blonde hair looked like a movie star.

'Just back from the metropolis,' she said.

'Metropolis?' Cat asked.

'The nearest town. First time I've been there. Thought I should check it out, see if it's got a dance hall, multiplex, bowling alley and so on.'

'And?'

'It has a café, a police house and a small row of shops.'

'Including a flower shop?'

There was a nice bunch of flowers on the passenger seat.

'To brighten up the library,' Miss Piper said.

Speechless took me aside. 'Do we tell her about...you know?'

'Tell me about what?' Miss Piper asked him.

'Loudmouth,' I said.

'Me?' said Miss P.

'No, the mental giant here. He forgot you can hear him too.'

'What are you wondering if you should tell me?' she asked Speechless.

Before he could answer, Cat gripped his arm, said, 'Nothing, nothing at all,' and marched him away from the road.

'Has something happened that I should know about?' Miss Piper asked me.

I shrugged, and hurried after the others. When I caught up with them, Cat was saying to Speechless, very quietly, 'How can we tell her the bloke she fancies killed the real Jack Toliver, hypnotised students for their powers, and has turned into a painting of himself?'

'She'll have to hear sooner or later,' I said. 'Some of it anyway.'

'Not from me, she won't,' said Cat.

29

I was in the games room playing myself at chess and in danger of losing because I had no idea how chess works. Cat and Speechless had wanted to carry on talking about what happened at the chapel, about Jack and all, but I needed a break from all that, and them. I should have known it wouldn't last.

'Dax, come to the bedcells.'

Speechless. In my head. I didn't answer. Not much point really, seeing as he wasn't in the room and couldn't hear me.

Minutes passed.

'Dax. Meet Cat and me at the bedcells. We need to talk.'

You might, I thought. I don't. So I didn't move. Well, I did. I moved one of the little pieces with a crown on its head. Then I moved one of the different colour ones with a crown, and soon they were fighting. One of the crowned ones was beating the other senseless when a terrifying creature with long pointed teeth dripping blood charged across the room at me.

'Dax! Now! Important!'

I jumped, sending the chess board flying. Others in the room jumped too, but because of me, not the terrifying creature. They hadn't seen the creature because it had only been in my head. Besides, it had vanished now.

I ran out of the room, and upstairs. In the passageway that separates the girls and boys bedcells, I found several kids looking either shocked or alarmed. Cat and Speechless were with them. I marched up to Speechless and thumped him on the shoulder.

'Ow!'

'I told you not to *do* that!'

'Well you wouldn't come,' he said, gripping his shoulder.

'I was busy,' I said.

One of the alarmed-looking kids – a girl – came up to us.

'Did you put that monster in my head?' she asked Speechless.

'Yes. Sorry. I was trying to put it in Dax's. Don't know how to focus it yet.'

'Well learn!' she said, and thumped his other shoulder.

'Ow!'

'That goes for me too,' said a boy, approaching with a raised fist.

Cat stepped in front of Speechless. 'It's just a blip. He'll get it sorted.'

'He'd better.'

The boy and the other kids walked off, grumbling.

'What's so urgent that you have to pull the monster trick?' I asked Speechless.

He was holding both of his thumped shoulders

and looking very sorry for himself, so Cat answered for him. 'We need to find out which member of staff was Jack's partner in crime.'

'Partner in crime?'

'He said he knew nothing about genetics and that he was working with the discoverer of the Lomas Gene, and—'

'I don't think he actually said that.'

'He hinted at it, and that's all we've got to go on. If he wasn't making it up and Lomas is here, he would have to have a different identity so no one would suspect him.'

'He could be anyone,' I said. 'He might be disguised as one of the people we don't see much – a dinner lady or cleaner, say. Even Mr Banner.'

'He can't be Mr Banner,' said Speechless, still holding his shoulders and looking pained. 'Jack made him shrink, and he was thinking of killing him.'

'They could have had a falling out.'

'Mr Banner a super smart genetic scientist?' said Cat. 'No, can't see it.'

'We didn't suspect Jack either,' I reminded her.

'We really should stop calling him Jack,' said Speechless.

'We should, but I've forgotten the name he gave us.'

'Bernard. Bernard Marx.'

'I still think it's one of the super tutors,' said Cat. 'Which means Mr Cosmo or Gladhusband. Jack made fun of me when I suggested them, but that could have been a smokescreen.'

I shook my head. 'Can't be one of them. The four super tutors have known one another for years, since they were ordinary teachers. If one of them was a top scientist the others would know.'

'We need a photo,' Cat said.

'What of?'

'Reinhardt Lomas. If he's such a big man in his field there must be a snap of him online.'

'Online,' I said. 'Brilliant. What do you suggest, wait till next Saturday when we're next allowed in the Com Centre?'

'No, we use the computer in the library.'

'It's Sunday. The library won't be open.'

'Not officially. But Miss Piper seems keen to make

it available to students whenever they want a book or information.'

'I thought you didn't want to bump into her now that Jack's gone.'

'I feel sorry for her,' Cat said, 'but identifying Lomas is more important than personal feelings, even hers. Anyway, she'll have heard that he's left by now.'

'Left?' I said. 'He didn't actually leave. And we're the only ones who know what happened – unless the people who went to the remains of the chapel after us recognised him in the painting.'

'They wouldn't have recognised him. The place had just collapsed. It was all rubble and dust amid the mist. But if anyone did see him in the painting, they would only think it looked a bit like him, not that it was him. Well, I mean. Who would ever think that?'

'So how would Miss Piper have heard that he's no longer at Scragmoor?'

'There was a note. Pushed under the door of my dad's study.'

'A note?'

'From Jack.'

'From Jack? Jack wrote a note? What did it say?'

'Tell him,' Cat said to Speechless.

'My shoulders hurt,' he replied.

'Yeah, yeah. Tell him what the note said.'

'I get no sympathy,' said Speechless. 'I get thumped, I get shouted at, and no one cares.'

'We care,' said Cat. 'Deeply. Now tell him or I'll thump you myself.'

He sighed. 'It said something like "Dear Dr Withering, I'm sorry but I have to tender my resignation, effective immediately, because of a devastating family bereavement, Jack."'

'Tell him about the PS,' Cat said.

'The PS said: "You might want to take a look in the room under the old chapel. I planned to do some fun experiments there to help the students, but I have to rush, sorry again."'

'Jack wrote *that*?' I said. 'When?'

'About two hours ago,' said Cat.

'Two hours? But that's...'

'Impossible? Yes.'

'So...'

She nodded at Speechless, and I finally cottoned on.

'You should have seen it,' said Cat. 'Work of art. Total work of art. No one would know a kid wrote it.'

'It was her idea,' Speechless said to me.

'But what was the point?' I asked.

'The point,' said Cat, 'was to explain Jack not being around all of a sudden. If he'd vanished without a word people would wonder why, and where he'd gone, and even if no one suspected anything bad the police might have been called, and that wouldn't have done anyone any good. This way, Jack's given a reason for being out of the picture – even though he's very much in one now – and no one will be suspicious about anything.'

'What if someone realises it wasn't his handwriting?'

'They won't,' said Speechless. 'I saw his writing once. That's all I needed.'

'The thing is,' said Cat, 'everyone on the staff's bound to have heard about Jack quitting by now, including Miss Piper, who could be feeling pretty down as she was so obviously sweet on him. However, we have to run the risk of her being all tearful because we need a picture of Lomas so we can identify the person he's pretending to be and stop him carrying on Jack's evil work.'

'I don't see how he could carry on,' I said. 'Jack was the one who put the kids in a trance, and the beans have been spilled about the room under the chapel now. Without Jack and the room where Essence of Gene was extracted, what can Lomas do?'

'Maybe nothing, but we can't take any chances. Also, if we don't find out if he's at Scragmoor I for one will never trust another adult here. Even the dinner ladies.'

On the way to the library we passed a few teachers. They looked very serious. Sad, even. Sad about Jack leaving? Maybe. Or maybe they just didn't like Sunday afternoons.

The door of the library was closed. Cat knocked anyway. No answer.

'Told you,' I said.

She tried the handle. The door opened. She blew on her fingernails and buffed them up on her chest.

We looked in. No one there. But the place was
a mess. One of the bookshelves had fallen over, or
been pulled, and there were books all over the floor.
The flowers Miss Piper had bought were also on the
floor, scattered, like they'd been thrown down and
jumped on.

'Looks like someone really lost it,' said Cat.

'Miss Piper?' I said.

'If it was her, she must be even more upset than I thought she'd be.'

'Maybe the bookshelf toppled as she came in, and she threw the flowers in the air in shock and ran out,' Speechless said.

'Closing the door behind her?'

'Force of habit. Unless someone else did...'

Cat went to the computer on the desk and touched the keyboard. A sudden glow on her face showed that the screen had come to life. We joined her as she sat down, leaning over on each side of her. She typed 'lomas gene' into a browser and links with the name Lomas and the word gene in them came up, but none had both of them together.

'The Lomas Gene's supposed to be a closely guarded secret,' I said.

'There's probably an SH1 gagging order on it,' said Speechless.

'OK, so now what?' Cat asked.

'Type Reinhardt Lomas,' I said.

'How do you spell Reinhardt?'

We weren't sure, but we got close enough for the search engine to find the name for us. The full name, with a link. A Wikipedia page came up with info about Reinhardt Lomas but nothing about the gene he discovered, just background stuff about him being a prominent geneticist. There was a picture, though. Him standing with seven people who were working under him when it was taken a couple of years earlier. The picture's caption said, 'Reinhardt Lomas and his team', with the names of the others too. Even without the names it would have been obvious which was Professor Lomas. He stood in the middle and looked in charge.

And we'd never seen him before.

But then Cat gasped.

And so did I.

And Speechless.

We were still gaping at the picture of Lomas and his team when the door opened and Mr Ruffalo looked in.

'Miss Piper hasn't gone already, has she?' he asked.

We looked up. But only Cat could find her voice.

'Gone?' It came out more like a squeak.

'Oh, you haven't heard? Her mother's fallen downstairs and she has to go and look after her because there's no one else. First Jack, now Miss Piper, both on the same day. Such a shame. Lovely woman.'

He left us, and Cat said, in a faint voice, 'She's gone.'

'She might not have, yet,' said Speechless.

Cat closed the browser and we left the room, only just managing not to crash into Mr Banner right outside.

'Watch where you're going,' he growled.

'Someone got up on the wrong side of the tor,' Cat said to his back as he went on his unmerry way.

In the lobby we found Mrs Withering and some of the teachers jamming the front door space, looking out. As we went up behind them we heard one of them say, 'I don't get it, he left his Harley, how did he...?'

Speechless slapped his forehead, which meant 'How could we have forgotten the bike?'

We eased our way through the little crowd and

went down into the courtyard. Over where the cars and Jack's motorbike were parked, Dr Withering, Mrs Page-Turner and Mr Gladhusband stood by Miss Piper's bright little car. She was in the driver's seat, talking to them, and for once she wasn't smiling. We had a quick parley between ourselves, and walked quickly across the courtyard and through the gateless gateposts. Outside, we ran to the tor where Mr Banner had been converted into a very small person, went behind it, and waited.

'Here she comes,' said Cat in a minute or two.

'If we're going to leap out,' Speechless said, 'give her time to brake. We don't want tyre tracks up our chests.'

We waited till the car was about twenty metres short of us, then ran out waving our arms. Miss Piper braked. In time.

She leaned out. She had her sunglasses on again, though it wasn't as bright as the last time we saw her in them.

'Still not smiling,' Speechless said quietly – but not quietly enough as Miss Piper could hear him in her head.

'I've had sad news,' she said as we joined her.

'We heard,' said Cat. 'Will you be back?'

'Unfortunately, no. My mum's had quite a tumble.'

'Of course. Your mother. She'll be needing you, won't she, Miss...Oleck?'

Miss Piper drew a breath, then let it out slowly.

'Where did you...?'

'We saw your picture,' Cat said.

'My picture?'

'Computer in the library. You and Professor Lomas's other assistants.'

At this Miss Piper's mouth twisted like she was biting down on something nasty.

'Assistant! I was the brightest one there. The brightest, best qualified, most skilled. Lomas was project head, so it was his name that was attached to the gene that I – I *alone* – discovered.'

'*You* discovered the Lomas Gene?' I said.

'Discovered it and did all the most intuitive practical work on it. I know more about that gene than anyone else alive.'

'Did you kill someone to get their job here too?' Speechless asked.

236

'Kill someone?'

'Like Jack did.'

'Oh, he told you, did he? When did he say that?'

'Just before he' – Speechless glanced at Cat and me – 'left us.'

Miss Piper shook her head. 'I passed myself off as a supremely competent and amiable librarian and wowed them at the interview. I've always known which buttons to press.'

'You sure knew which of ours,' said Cat. 'We thought you were the best.'

'I am the best – at what I do, what I know.'

'You also know how to put on an act, like Jack. Or should I say Bernard?'

'He told you that too, did he? What a fool.'

'Fool? We thought you were an item, or soon would be.'

'An item! Me with an IQ of 165, him an airhead with outrageously whitened teeth who takes nothing seriously?'

'So there was never anything between you?'

'Hardly. All Bernie had to do was put the kids in a trance and keep them there while I performed the procedure, then make them all sunny and smiley once they were well away from the room. It was just a game to him, I know that now. All my careful planning, all the subterfuge and effort, and he takes what he thinks he needs and leaves a note telling everyone about the room I had him equip for me.'

'There isn't much equipment there,' I said.

'There doesn't need to be if you know what you're doing.' She twisted her mouth again. 'I don't know where he's gone – or how, without that damn bike of his – but I'll track him down, and when I do...'

238

We couldn't see her eyes behind the shades, but you got the idea they would be pretty narrow right now. I noticed something else too. On the back seat beside her suitcase lay a laptop and a thermos flask.

'It was you who drained off the essence then,' I said.

'Essence?' she said.

'Of Lomas Gene.'

She looked surprised for a sec, then laughed. The laugh sounded genuine, like the laugh of the Miss Piper we'd liked so much.

'Essence of Gene,' she said. 'A line I spun him which he was dim-witted enough to accept. There is no "essence". The stuff I gave Bernie to drink was cheap cough mixture laced with tiny samples of the Gene's properties. If he thinks the silly little powers they gave him will get him anywhere away from here – or will even last – he's in for a very big disappointment.'

'How did you get the powers from the students if not the way Bernie thought?' Speechless asked.

'Oh, you'd like to know that, would you?'

'Well yes, actually. Was it through the arm?'

The woman we'd known as Miss Piper, but now

knew to be called Miss Oleck, smiled, but not kindly.

'Let's just say that I've formulated a highly focused copy-and-paste process, and leave it at that, shall we?'

'Have you got any powers or was it just him?' Cat asked her.

'Since you're so interested,' Miss Oleck said, 'I have just one at present. I intended to take my time acquiring others while getting my feet under Scragmoor's table. So much for long-term planning. That idiot's betrayal has changed everything.'

'So you won't be getting any more?' I said. 'Powers, I mean.'

The woman in the fancy little car laughed again, but this time it was a cold, hard laugh.

'Out there,' she said, 'beyond this abominable place, there are almost two hundred other kids with the gene I discovered – and I have all their addresses.'

'Is that the new plan then?' Cat asked. 'Go after some of the others?'

'Oh, indeed. But first, there's a certain individual who must learn the folly of sidelining Glenda Oleck.'

'You mean Jack? Bernard?'

'Oh, no, he's nothing. His time will come, but first I must deal with the man who stole the credit due to me.'

'You mean Professor Lomas?' Miss Oleck's smile said it all. 'What are you going to do to him?'

The lady lowered her sunglasses and peered over the top of them. There was no smile in her eyes. No kindness at all.

'I'm in two minds about the method, but only one of us will leave that meeting place alive. I might even use the single power I have at present. There would be some poetic justice in that, after all.'

'What's the single power?' I asked.

Miss Oleck hesitated, then said: 'Why don't I show you?'

She adjusted her sunglasses, opened the door, and got out. She looked the same as ever – nice face, good hair, cheerful clothes – but now that we knew who she really was – and what – we couldn't help but back off a little.

'You must forgive the crassness of this,' she said. 'It isn't something I would do, ordinarily.'

'Crassness?' I asked.

'Yes. Far from ladylike.'

Having no idea what to expect, we just stood there, waiting. Then Glenda Oleck cleared her throat, swallowed hard, and began to spit.

Yes, spit.

She spat further and faster than anyone I ever saw, one gob after another, rat-a-tat-tat, spatter-spat-spat, each one hitting the ground around our feet, so hard and close that right away we were dancing and dodging, like you do when bullets fly at your feet.

Yes, bullets.

That's what she was spitting. Solid, lethal bullets. I knew this because one of them bounced and hit my leg, spinning me round, and when I looked I saw that it was bleeding. Not much, the spit-bullet had only grazed me, but a bleed's a bleed.

'Stop!' we yelled. 'Stop! Stop!'

And she did.

'Don't worry,' she said, 'I'm not going to kill you. I could, very easily, I tested it to good effect earlier. Or perhaps I should,' she added thoughtfully. 'It's tempting, believe me, after having to be so sweet to you brats these past weeks.'

'You tested that power?' Cat said. 'When? Where? What on?'

Miss Oleck looked at her. 'When? Earlier today. That was my real reason for going to town today.'

'You mean you tested it on people?'

'No, no. Imagine the fuss that would have caused. No, on the way back. There are a lot of animals on the moor. Ponies, goats, sheep.'

'You shot ponies, goats and sheep?'

'Spat, not shot. Though the result was the same.'

'You killed defenceless animals to see if that power worked?' This was Speechless.

'All in the glorious cause of science.' Miss Oleck chuckled humourlessly.

It was about then that something new happened. While getting over being grazed by the spit-bullet, something rose in my throat, making me gulp. I thought I was going to throw up. But I didn't throw up. Not exactly.

I began to spit, long and hard and fast.

Now it was someone else who was hopping and dodging spit-bullets smacking the ground around her feet.

'How do you do that?' Miss Oleck cried, dancing.

I couldn't tell her. Couldn't say anything. When bullet-hard pellets of spit leap out of your mouth at such a rate there isn't a lot of room for words too.

The final straw for her seemed to be when her sunglasses flew off. 'Right!' she said. 'If that's the way it's to be!'

Then she was spitting again – but so was I, at her – and all four of us were hopping about, though we had to jump higher than her because she didn't seem bothered any more about hitting the ground. It was Speechless who decided to try and put an end to this. He ran towards her. Not straight at her, but out a little, and round, to try and avoid the spray of mouth pellets. She saw him coming and had to flip her head from front to side and back again to make sure all three of us were held at bay, but when he was near enough he jumped at her, arms over his head to protect himself, and sent Miss Oleck flying. She went right over onto her back and when she got up she was no longer spitting, just cursing. She ran at Speechless, who lay where he'd fallen after throwing himself at her, and kicked him hard.

'Wretch!' she screamed.

Then she leapt into her car.

'Don't be surprised if we meet again,' she shouted at us. 'Only next time I'll have more powers. And remember this. I dispose of my enemies!'

Dry-mouthed from all the bullet spitting, I stood watching her drive away in her sweet, flowery little car.

'Dax,' Cat said from somewhere behind me.

I turned round. She was kneeling beside Speechless, who wasn't moving. She had her ear to his mouth.

'He's not breathing,' she said.

'What?'

She felt his neck. Then one of his wrists.

'No pulse.'

'What do you mean?'

'I mean she's killed him,' Cat said.

'*What!*'

'He's dead, Dax. Speechless is dead.'

31

There was a hole in his shirt, and a spreading red stain. We crouched beside his body, across from one another, one on each side of him.

'Stupid little idiot,' I said.

Cat stared at me with very watery eyes.

'Dax, how can you say such a thing?'

'I can say it because he didn't have to do that.'

'He saved our lives,' she said.

'Yeah, well who asked him to?'

But my eyes were watery too, which made me angry with myself as well as Speechless. I dashed the tears away with my sleeve while Cat put a hand on his chest, right over the red patch, like if she couldn't see it, it wouldn't exist.

'So much for super powers,' she said. 'A lousy, stinking super power killed our friend.'

Neither of us knew what to do next. We might have stayed there quite a while, just squatting by him, saying things that didn't mean anything, change anything. But it was Cat who finally did something, and – like me when the bullets started spitting from my mouth – it wasn't something she planned or even knew she could to.

It started with her eyes.

They didn't get any greener or brighter like they did in the dark, but went a sort of a pale cream colour, and then the pale creamness spread from her eyes through her face, down her neck, into the hand that lay on Speechless's chest, and then...it drained out of her and into him, like it was filling him up, and he jerked suddenly, and gasped, and Cat fell back in shock. I fell back too, but not before seeing that the hand she'd placed over the red stain had fallen open and in her palm lay something bullet-shaped.

Seconds passed, and during those seconds Cat's natural colour came back, and so did Speechless's. Then Speechless blinked, and sat up.

'Did I stop her?' he asked in a dazed sort of way.

'What?' I said, staring at him.

'Miss Piper. Miss Oleck. Did I stop her?'

'Yes. You stopped her.'

He looked around. 'Has she gone then?'

'Yeah. Like a speeding spit bullet. Why didn't you give her the scary mind monster treatment?'

'She was spitting like a crazy person. If I'd panicked her she might have hit someone.'

'She did hit someone.'

I nodded at his chest. He looked down. Saw the red patch.

'My shirt!'

'Not just your shirt.'

'Dax!' hissed Cat, getting to her feet.

But it was too late. I'd said it. And Speechless was opening his shirt. He stared at the little circle in his chest. The bullet-shaped hole, which...had healed over.

'Me?' He said. 'She shot me?'

'Not fatally,' said Cat, shoving the spit-bullet into the ground, out of sight.

'I'll be scarred for life.'

'Better than dead for life,' I said.

Cat came over to me. 'Don't you dare tell him,' she whispered.

'Why not?'

'Because he probably wouldn't want to know that

he'd died and been brought back to life. Promise me, Dax.'

I shrugged an OK.

She smiled happily. 'Not just glow-in-the-dark eyes then. I have a proper power. A useful one.'

'Looks like it,' I said.

'What are you two whispering about?' Speechless asked.

'Nothing,' said Cat.

'No, come on, tell me.'

'If we wanted you to know, we would,' I said, 'and we don't, so keep your nose out.'

'Look, I'll see you back at the school,' Cat said.

'Why, where are you going?' I asked.

'There are dead animals out there. I have to see if I can do anything for them.'

'What could you do for dead animals?' Speechless asked.

'They might not all be dead.'

'They could be miles from here,' I said.

'I don't care. I have to go and see.'

'You can't go out there on your own. People get lost on the moor. Things happen to them.'

'If I'm not back by nightfall,' she said, walking away, 'gather the heroes.'

She was laughing as she set off.

32

Two days later I had a thought about the painted people wall. Like I've said, the fresco was painted on part of the high wall that surrounds the school, which is why it was the only bit of the chapel left standing after the last section of roof fell in. My thought was that if the people in the fresco had started to come to life when our Lomas Genes appeared on the scene, might there not be more to them now than just paint on a flat surface? More bulk, I mean. Like on the other side of the wall as well as the ex-chapel side?

The only parts of the wall around the school that we generally saw from the main building were either from upstairs windows or the courtyard. The back of the section the chapel had stood against was out near the old north wing. The north wing had no roof at all, not a shred of one, and all five floors of the six storeys above the ground had been removed for safety's sake, so we weren't forbidden to go there. If we hardly ever *did* go there it was because there was nothing to do there, nothing to even see. But I had a reason to go there now, and that's where I headed.

The north wing still had all four of its very tall walls, but the big doorway that had once been the entry point from outside (or exit point from inside) had no door these days, so you could just walk out. About fifty metres the other side of the doorway there was a broad batch of thick, high bushes that had been let go since the prison and museum days. The roof of the chapel used to rise above the bushes. You couldn't see it now, of course, because it wasn't there any more, but the back of the bit of wall the fresco was painted on stood behind those bushes. Thick as they were, I managed to squeeze between them and the wall to the part the chapel had stood against. I knew I'd reached the spot when I saw that I'd been right about the painted people developing some bulk. They were coming through on this side of the wall too.

They were in the wall now, not just painted on the other side of it!

The paintwork looked fainter here than on the chapel side, but there they were, all nineteen of them, in the same trudging pose. Some of them were looking straight ahead, others showed the backs of their heads, and none of them moved – till I got very close. Then a couple of them shivered, then another one or two, like they were waking up. But only one head moved.

Jack's.

He turned it to look at me, like he'd sensed me. The puzzlement had gone. Now he looked angry. Furious. And his fury was directed at me. He opened his mouth, and I thought he was going to scream at me or demand to be let out of the wall, but I stepped sharply back, into one of the bushes, and he froze again, mouth wide, eyes glaring. The other movers also froze. Further proof, if any was needed, that it was the presence of the Gene that gave the painted people life.

I left Jack like that, faint but glaring, about to shout, and vowed never to go near that bit of wall again, either side of it. If every boy or girl with the Gene kept away from it, the people in the wall would never move again, and someday – maybe – they would fade to nothing, on both sides, taking Bernard Marx with them.

I went back through the north wing and into the main building. I was just turning a corner into the lobby when who should come the other way but Dr Withering. Crash. Full-frontal collision.

'It's all right, Forty-one, don't apologise,' he said.

'That goes for you too,' I said.

'But as you're here, would you join me in my study for a minute? There's something I want to talk to you about. And ask you.'

'If it's to clean your car or your shoes,' I replied, 'I want the money up front.'

He didn't laugh. He led the way to his study, held his door open for me, and closed it smartly once I was inside. Then he went to his desk and sat down behind it.

'Don't stand on ceremony,' he said, waving at the chair across from him.

Throwing myself into it, I said: 'What's up, Doc?'

He sighed. 'Will the novelty of saying that never wear off?'

'I'll let you know,' I said.

He growled deep in his throat, like he often does when I'm about, and said, 'I've been getting mixed reviews about you.'

'Yeah? The singing voice or the impressions of you?'

'Some say that you have a power.'

'Some say all sorts of things. You don't want to listen.'

'Would you care to tell me about it?'

'There's nothing to tell.'

He paused, then said: 'You don't make it easy, do you, Forty-one?'

'Make what easy?'

'Do you still not like it here?'

'It's an ex-prison where people were sent to rot or be hanged by the neck until dead – what's not to like?'

'So you're still keen to leave?'

'Well...' I dried up.

'You didn't have any trouble answering that a few weeks ago,' he said.

'Forty-one days actually.'

'Oh, you've been counting, and today is Hero 41's forty-first day, is it? What a coincidence.'

'I'm no hero,' I said.

'You could be, one day. A real hero, doing something worthwhile.'

'Why would I want to be a hero? Why would anyone who doesn't live in a comic?'

He sat back in his chair and eye-contacted me, so silently and for so long that I almost gave in. Almost. He was the first to blink.

'When I was approached to head this project,' he said at last, 'I realised that some students would have a little trouble accepting their unique potential, to say nothing of adjusting to life in surroundings such as these. So I told SH1 that I would give my students time to get used to everything, then ask those who seemed less at ease than the rest if they wished to stay or go.'

He leaned forward, elbows on his desk.

'Hence this little chat.'

'You're actually giving me a go-or-stay choice?' I asked. 'This isn't a trick?'

'I don't do tricks, Dax.'

I felt my eyebrows rise. 'I don't think you've ever used my name before.'

'Then I'll have to make sure it doesn't become a habit, won't I? I could easily do that if I never saw you again.'

'So you want me to go.'

'What I want,' he said, 'is for you to say what you want.'

'I want a bed.'

'A bed?'

'I've mentioned it before a couple of times.'

'You have. And as it happens, that's another thing I wanted to mention.'

'You've got one for me?'

'In a way. By tomorrow there'll be a spare bunk.'

'A spare? How come?'

'Byron Flood's leaving us.'

'Byron? No. Why?'

'He's unhappy about his power, which seems to be growing by the day. It doesn't work when he's away from the rest of you, he says, but when you're around – even if it's just one of you – he can hear the tiniest thing. So he's asked to go home in order to get back to...well, normal, I suppose.'

'I asked that on day one, but you wouldn't let me go.'

'You didn't have a legitimate excuse. Byron does. His sanity might be at stake. So what do you say?'

'You mean I'd have to move in with Howley Marsh?'

'Would that be a problem?'

'I've kind of got used to Speechless.'

'Well, I can't organise everything for you,' he said sharply.

'Hey,' I said. 'Marcus and Howley. They're mates. Maybe Marcus would take Byron's bunk.'

'You can sort that out among yourselves. I just wanted to tell you that from tomorrow you have a bunk if you want it. But the question remains: do you want it or would you prefer to leave? If the latter, I won't block your departure this time.'

'If I went too, you'd only have thirty-nine students.'

'Not for long. There's no shortage of others with the Lomas Gene. We can take our pick. If it's up to me I'll be sure to look for someone with a decent attitude next time.'

'Ah, go on,' I said. 'You'd miss me, you know you would.'

He sighed again. 'Do you, or do you not, wish to stay at Scragmoor?'

I shrugged. 'Might as well.'

'That's very big of you,' he said.

'I know. It's the way I am. Is that it then? Can I go now?'

'Oh, feel free.'

I got up and headed for the door, but stopped as I reached it.

'With Byron gone and me staying you'll be down to the forty students you wanted in the first place,' I said.

'Yes? So?'

'You won't be able to call me Forty-one any more.'

He peered at me from under his ridiculously hairy eyebrows.

'To me, my lad, you'll always be Forty-one.'

'The unwanted extra, you mean?'

'You might very well think that,' he said. 'I couldn't possibly comment. Shut the door on your way out, Hero 41.'

Funny thing is, there was a smile on his face when he said that.

Don't miss Dax's first adventure at
SCRAGMOOR PRIME!

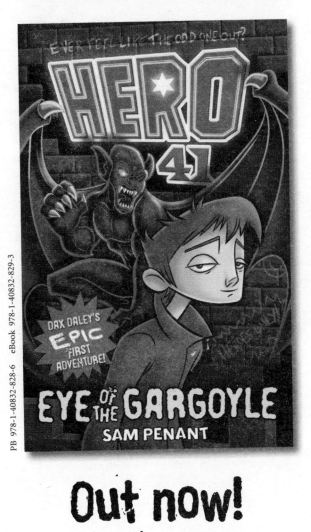

Out now!

Read on for a sneak peek…

I didn't know it yet, but I was on my way to prison. By bus. My parents had arranged it.

Some parents.

It was a long journey. Felt like days. There'd been other passengers most of the way, but when I woke from my latest doze I found that I was alone. Apart from the driver, that is. I woke this time because the bus had stopped and the driver had spoken. He'd turned in his seat and was looking along the empty bus, at me, all bundled up at the back.

'I said this is as far as I go, son,' he said.

I looked out of the window. There was nothing there. Just old brown land. No buildings, no trees, nothing. I looked out of other windows. Same.

'As far as you go?'

He beckoned, and I slid out of my seat, lugged my suitcase down the aisle. At the front he pointed through his windscreen at an ancient stone beside the road. There were three words cut into the stone.

TWO MILE POINT

'What does that mean?'

'It means that no one born round here, like I was, goes beyond that sign unless they really have to.'

'Why not? The road does.'

'The road's not gonna get any bad luck, is it?'

'Is that what you think will happen to you if you do?'

'I'm not taking any chances. Out you get.'

'How far is it?' I asked.

'Couple of miles, like the sign says. You'll be there in no time. Luck, kid.'

And then I was outside and the doors were closed and the bus was reversing onto the rough ground, and then it was off, and I was alone.

The view wasn't improved by being in it rather than on the other side of a window. It rose and fell and was misty round the edges, and there were all these rocks heaped on top of one another, and there were animals here and there – goats, ponies, a few sheep – standing in small groups like they were chatting about something on last night's telly.

But that was it.

I set off along the road, suitcase banging against my leg, switching hands every now and then to give it a chance to bang the other leg. They might at least have given me a case with wheels on, I thought. I meant my parents, of course. The ones behind all this. The day they told me was still vivid in my mind.

'You're sending me to *boarding* school?' I cried. 'What am I, Harry Potter all of a sudden?'

'If only,' said Dad. 'We could do with a little magic in our lives.'

'Your father's joking,' said Mum. 'This is an opportunity for you, Dax.'

'Opportunity? Being sent away from home is an opportunity? What have I done to deserve it? Is it the window? I told the school governors it was an accident. Even offered to get you to pay for it.'

'It's nothing to do with the window and this isn't a punishment. It's an exciting prospect. You'll be one of Scragmoor Prime's first pupils.'

'Scragmoor Prime? I hate it already, and I don't

want to be one of its first pupils. I want to stay where I am. I'm happy there.'

'Happy?' said Dad. 'That's news. All we ever get from you about King's Landing is complaints.'

'Well of course! It's school. Nobody says good things about school. That's no reason to take me out of it and send me... Oh, wait. I get it. You want rid of me. Want me out of the way so you can have a nice quiet Dax-free life. Well, thanks a lot. It's been so good having you two for parents.'

'Don't get upset, darling,' Mum said, reaching for my cheek.

I reared back. 'Don't you darling me, treacherous parent!'

'You should be proud,' said Dad. 'Scragmoor doesn't accept just anyone. They actually asked for you.'

'Asked for me? Asked for *me*? How do they even know I exist?'

'Ah. Well. Remember last term, having to lick an envelope with your name on it and hand it to your teacher?'

'Sure. I cut my tongue on it. Every kid in the

country had to do it – lick an envelope, not cut their tongue. Something to do with supplying a DNA sample for government databanks.'

'It wasn't for databanks, Dax. It was for analysis.'

'Analysis?'

'They say a new gene's been identified – quite a rare one – and the genetic code of every boy and girl your age has been examined to see which among you possesses it.'

'And I do?'

Mum and Dad looked at one another, then beamed at me with shining eyes.

'You do!' said Mum.

I did not beam back. My eyes did not shine. 'What is this gene?'

'It's a secret,' said Dad.

'You mean you're not going to tell me?'

'I mean *top* secret. Official. Even we don't know.'

'Oh, wonderful. Terrific. So I've got this rare gene that could make me grow two heads, maybe three, and you're sending me away to give this school with the horrible name a chance to help them *develop*?'

'Exactly!' said Mum.

'Look,' I said. 'Tell you what,' I said. 'I'll behave in class. I'll work harder. I'll even stop answering my teachers back. How's that?'

Dad sighed. 'Dax, you were born misbehaving, slacking and answering back. It's who you are. Can't see you changing now.'

'I can try,' I said desperately.

'Sorry, too late. We've signed the papers agreeing to you continuing your education at Scragmoor.'

'Whoa,' I said. 'Hang on.' There was something suspicious about this. 'Is there something in it for you?'

'Apart from the money, you mean?' said Dad.

Mum glared at him. 'We weren't going to mention that,' she said.

I stared from one to the other of them, and back again.

'They *paid* you? You *sold* me to this school?'

Dad laughed. 'No, no, no. Admittedly, the grant will clear all our debts at a stroke, but we were thinking of you, Dax. You. Your future.'

My future?

Oh boy.

They had no *idea* what was in store for me at Scragmoor Prime.

Who could *ever* have guessed that?